The Disappearing Diamond

Glen Blackwell

Cover illustration by Anastasiia Frizen

Copyright © 2023 Glen Blackwell

Published by Zoetrope Books 2023
Suffolk, England

All rights reserved

A CIP catalogue record for this book is available from the British Library

ISBN : 978-1-8383252-6-8

www.zoetropebooks.com

For Lou

Thank you for planting the seed

1

Visiting The Museum

Emmie turned to Jack with a barely suppressed grin. Her friend looked quite ridiculous in the oversize cap, which completely covered his orange hair. It kept slipping over his eyes, causing him to push it further back on his head. Each time he did so, his eyes narrowed a little – the only sign of irritation at the continued need to adjust it. He was such a clown, Emmie thought – choosing a hat which didn't fit, just because he thought it went with the waistcoat his mum had picked out from a charity shop for him. Neither really matched the dark trousers he wore which were too short for his tall frame, but Jack didn't seem to care – he thought he looked the part, and that was all that mattered. The school trip to the Victoria and Albert Museum was a treat after learning about the Victorian period all term long. It was good to see some real things from that time instead of just hearing about them in the classroom.

Turning away before Jack noticed her staring, Emmie gazed around the large room. It was more of a gallery really, with bookshelves along one wall and display cabinets along the other. There were more cabinets running down the middle, each containing several different objects. Above them was a mezzanine with black metal railings running around it, in front of yet more bookshelves. The air had a curious aroma; dust and old books, mixed with the smell of fresh paint. It felt brighter than the last time they had visited too.

'Clonk!' A sign on the edge of one of the cabinets fell to the floor and Jack bent down to pick it up. There was a small cheer from the children nearest to him who had seen Jack accidentally knock it off with his elbow. Emmie rolled her eyes – he was always involved in some drama or other, and it was often her who had to pick up the pieces.

The class were clustered in small groups around several cabinets in the room, listening to the museum guides and teachers describing some of the artefacts inside. In front of Emmie, sparkling in the carefully positioned light, was one of the largest gemstones she had ever seen. It was sitting on its edge, angled towards the visitors' gaze, and lying on a bed of purple velvet. The assembled children were captivated by the shimmering clear jewel - most of them only paying partial attention to the museum guide as they stared at the cabinet. He was describing how the diamond they were looking at was called the Koh-i-Noor and was one of the largest cut diamonds in the world. It was soon to be used in the upcoming coronation of the new king.

'Pretty, isn't it?' Jack said quietly at her side. He reached up to adjust his cap again as he spoke.

'Pretty?' replied Emmie slowly, twirling one of her dark plaits. 'That doesn't come close. It's amazing! I can't wait to see the diamond sparkling in the ceremony.' Emmie was a huge fan of all things royal and had persuaded her parents to get up early and watch next week's coronation in person.

'I bet it's worth millions...' Jack took half a step forward for a closer look.

As he approached the cabinet, the lights in the gallery gave a sudden flicker, and Jack turned to Emmie in surprise. 'Did I get too close?' he wondered out loud. Emmie didn't get a chance to answer, as an alarm started blaring out loudly above their heads, causing her to jump. She stared in horror at the cabinet, trying to see what might have caused the alarm to go off.

'What did you do?! Did you touch it?' she shouted at him over the noise. Jack shook his head, rooted to the spot and looking very pale. Emmie glanced worriedly around, expecting to see security guards rushing into the room, but everyone else seemed to be standing motionless, despite the cacophony around them. She looked left and right, her forehead furrowed by both the noise and the shock of how suddenly it had started.

'What's going on, Jack?' she shouted again, feeling really unsettled by their statuesque classmates. He had his hands over his ears now, in an attempt to block out the noise, and was staring down at his feet. She shoved him in the side, trying to get a reaction, but instead he brought his shoulders closer together and hunched his head forward.

Emmie was frantic now. 'Jack!' He shrugged her off, and then she felt a hand touch her arm gently. She whirled around and stared in surprise at the man in a long dark coat who stood before her. Their eyes locked and she involuntarily stepped back, almost crashing into Jack. Steadying herself in disbelief, she took a deep breath, before shutting her eyes and opening them again. He was still there, staring silently at her – a picture of calm in the middle of the aural chaos around them. 'You...' she said quietly, and the man nodded – presumably having read her lips as it was impossible to hear over the alarm.

He motioned to a doorway behind him, and Emmie's mind raced – was this really something she wanted to get involved with again? Their last encounter had been rather dramatic and, though she had been half-expecting to see the man again for a while, the manner of his appearance was still quite a surprise. She grabbed at Jack's arm and pulled, only succeeding in getting a shake of his head. 'JACK!' she tried again, putting her arms on his shoulders and trying to manoeuvre him to look at the man. He raised his head, instant recognition flashing across his face. Reluctantly, he held the man's gaze, chewing his lip as he did so.

The man leaned in close to them. 'I need your help again,' he said, trying to make himself heard above the din. He indicated the doorway behind him once more. 'Please?'

Jack slowly looked round at Emmie – he was still very pale, but there was a tiny glint of interest in his eyes too. He turned back to the room, seeing that the rest of the class were still immobile, seemingly frozen in time somehow. His eyes flicked to the cabinet with the gem which seemed to be the centre of all of this and let out a loud gasp – it was empty!

His heart beat faster – this was bad. It was one thing maybe setting an alarm off accidentally but being involved in a jewel disappearing – that was far worse! He glanced back at Emmie and the man, seeing him nodding to them as though he already knew somehow.

Jack nodded back, certain that the man's appearance at this moment was no coincidence. He reached out his hand to Emmie and stepped forward, feeling a mixture of apprehension and excitement at what might lie ahead. The man smiled at them, turned, and walked quickly through the doorway – the pair following behind. The next room was in semi-darkness as the windows were covered in large shutters, making it hard to see where they were going. Ahead of them, the faint outline of the man reached for a door handle and tugged it open, throwing a bright beam of light into their path.

As their eyes struggled to adjust, Emmie noticed that they were stepping through into the museum gift shop – its blue-painted walls covered in souvenirs, books and toys. A model of a red London bus sat on the shelf right in front of her, and seeing it gave her goosebumps. There was a clang as the door closed behind them and the sound of the alarm diminished. 'What's going on? Why are you here?' she asked the man, glad the ringing in her ears had largely stopped.

'We have to hurry,' he replied, dodging her question. 'You saw the diamond had disappeared – I need your help to find it in time for the coronation. It can't go ahead without the Koh-i-Noor – it's going to be mounted on the State crown for the ceremony. Something has happened in the past and I need you to find out what it is and put it right.'

Emmie gasped – no coronation? That would be terrible. 'Why us though?' she persisted.

'Because we can. I don't know why, but I think your friend probably does.' Jack joined in now. He was staring at the London bus model and remembering their unexpected trip back to the Blitz the year before.

'Tell us! If we're going to help you again, then we should at least know why.' Emmie stared at the man, a hint of annoyance in her expression.

'We haven't got any time now. Don't you remember what happens if things shift in the past when they aren't meant to? I'll explain everything when you get back. And I mean everything.' This last sentence hung in the air between them for a moment before Emmie slowly nodded. 'Excellent,' said the man, striding over to a fire door and throwing it open. 'Be quick, and good luck!'

Emmie and Jack stepped through the open doorway, blinking in the bright sunshine. Emmie turned to ask the man what he needed them to do when they found the diamond, only to come face-to-face with the door being firmly shut with a loud bang.

'What the—' managed Jack in a strangled voice behind her, as he gazed at the scene around them.

Horses Everywhere

Instead of a bustling London street, decorated with Union Jack bunting in readiness for the coronation, what they saw was totally different.

'Where are we?' asked Emmie in surprise. 'Or should I say – when are we?' She indicated the building behind them – the fire escape they'd passed through was no longer there, and instead a large townhouse stood in its place.

'So that's what was here before the museum,' Jack said quietly. 'Assuming we are still in London.' This had happened to them twice before now, and they always seemed to move in time but not location. He gazed further down the road, seeing that the houses grew denser, and the sky had turned a dirty grey colour.

Emmie stared up at him – the shock of the past few minutes not really having sunk in yet. 'Where do we go from here?' she asked. 'All we really know is that we need to find that diamond or the coronation won't be able to happen.' The responsibility of solving such an important problem suddenly felt very heavy.

'Why didn't your friend tell us some more before he slammed the door?' Jack replied.

'He's not my friend,' Emmie shot back, then paused – slightly taken aback at the strength of her reaction.

'Well, you seemed really keen to do what he said last time...'

Emmie looked at Jack – when she'd first encountered the mysterious time architect on Titanic, she'd been fearful of his cryptic comments. He had proven to be their saviour in the end though – guiding the friends home after they had saved Mary – the young girl they met on board. It had never been clear who he was though – the man seemed to know about their ability to move through time, but never explained how or why to them. On this occasion, however, he had dangled the carrot of an explanation when asking for their help. 'I think we have to trust him again,' she said, 'and we're here now anyway.' She was right – there was no obvious route back since the modern building they had just left had now vanished.

'What did he mean about things shifting in the past when they aren't meant to?' asked Jack.

'The butterfly effect, I guess,' Emmie replied. 'Don't you remember that penny from 1940 and all the fuss it caused?'

Jack's face paled. He remembered only too well the shock he had experienced when the world they knew seemed to have vanished before their eyes. He had learned very quickly that changing the past could have huge unintended consequences.

'Come on – let's see if we can work out where we actually are?' Emmie said as she hitched up her long skirt, trying not to trip over the hem. 'We can think of a plan whilst we walk.'

Jack followed Emmie along the pavement to their left, dodging pedestrians as they went. No-one seemed to pay them any attention, and he realised that their efforts at dressing up for the trip to the museum were probably helping them blend in. Reaching a road junction, they stopped in surprise at the scene in front of them.

Horses. Everywhere you looked there were horses. They were pulling every conceivable kind of wagon – from crowded omnibuses, with people fighting for space on the roof, to carts piled high with goods for market. In amongst them, men in flat caps pulled barrows – darting in and out of the heavy traffic. And the road – as well as thronging with people and vehicles, it was absolutely covered in horse droppings. The cobbled surface had virtually disappeared in some places, so deep was the manure.

Jack gagged, putting a hand to his mouth as the putrid smell hit the back of his throat. 'Urgh,' he grumbled through gritted teeth, 'this is grim.'

'It's got to be the Victorian period,' Emmie suggested, 'this much horse-drawn transport and all the soot and pollution too.' She stared around some more. 'I still think we're in London though.' Suddenly, her face lit up with excitement. 'Maybe we'll see Queen Victoria? I'd love that.'

It wasn't just the smell which was oppressive – the noise was something to behold too. A cacophony of shouting, neighing and the rumbling of carriage wheels made it feel quite disorientating to the pair. Looking across the junction, they saw why the horse-drawn traffic was so choked up – a cart had lost a wheel, and a group of men were trying to push it back to the kerb. There was a lot of angry, impatient shouting coming from the other road users, several of whom were trying to force a route through. Eventually the cart made way for some of the other traffic to pass, and a level of order was restored.

'At least this doesn't feel as dangerous as the Blitz,' Jack said. 'Still, I remember reading that there were lots of nasty diseases in Victorian times, so maybe it is after all...'

'Come on,' Emmie tugged at Jack's arm, 'let's keep moving.' They carried on along the pavement, trying to keep to the side away from the road as much as possible.

'Eels! Get your eels!' came a yell from a man with a small cart by the side of the road, causing Emmie to jump for the second time that day. He was wearing a tattered jacket and had a scarf around his neck, despite the warmth of the day. There was already a crowd of people surrounding him, yet he still shouted his wares as he served them. Emmie stretched to see the cups of eels being handed out, then turned back to Jack with a pale expression on her face.

'I'm not sure which is the most unpleasant – those eels or the smell of horse,' she whispered to Jack. 'They look really slimy!'

'You don't want me to buy you some then?' joked Jack, a wicked grin spreading over his face. He pretended to approach the seller, and Emmie tugged him back.

'No!' she hissed, 'don't waste your money.' Both friends suddenly froze and looked at each other – money... 'Do you actually have any money?' Emmie asked, patting her pockets and realising that their quest for the missing diamond might span several mealtimes.

'Umm, maybe...' replied Jack, putting his hand into his trousers and coming out with a couple of coins.

'Those might be a bit of a problem,' said Emmie quietly, seeing the shiny £2 coins Jack was holding. 'I don't think anyone is going to accept them.'

'It's ok – we'll pawn them,' Jack said confidently.

'Pawn? What do you mean?'

'Think of Cash Converters,' explained Jack. 'That shop exchanges money for things which have value – maybe they'll think these coins are worth something...'

'So, we just need to find a Victorian Cash Converters branch?'

'Which is called a pawn shop,' finished Jack. 'They have three golden balls outside as a sign. I'm sure we'll find one quite easily.'

Their conversation was abruptly stopped as a shout rang out further along the street. 'Quick, the peelers are coming!' People started running down the pavement, and Emmie noticed the eel seller hurriedly packing up his cart.

'What are peelers?' Jack asked, leaning in close to Emmie. A man knocked into them in his haste to get past, causing her to stagger against the fence behind the path.

'The police,' she muttered, quickly getting back to her feet and brushing down her skirt. 'Something's about to happen – I can feel it.' They walked swiftly away, carried along by the sea of people doing the same thing.

'In here!' Jack hissed, tugging Emmie's arm and steering her into a road which opened up to the side of them. She could see rows of houses lining either side of the road, with a green space and some trees in the middle.

'Look – Brompton Square! We are in London still,' she exclaimed excitedly – pointing at a sign high up on the first house as Jack dragged her past.

'I thought so,' replied Jack, 'that's good news.' He led them across to the grassed area and sat down by the side of a large oak tree. They had a view of the main road from here but were partially hidden unless anyone came right into the square itself. It turned out to be a good decision as three angry policemen appeared, chasing a man with a handcart who was dropping baskets and other items as he ran along the street. The dark-uniformed policemen were waving their batons angrily, trying to get the crowds of pedestrians out of their way and avoid having to run in the manure-filled road.

'I wonder what he's done wrong?' Emmie pondered. 'Those policemen are really cross.'

Jack nodded in agreement. 'Did you see how quickly the eel man packed up when he heard them coming? I wonder if they're not allowed to sell things on the street...'

'Shame – I was starting to feel a bit hungry,' Emmie joked, the shock of the policemen's appearance fading.

'Let's try and find that pawn shop and hopefully exchange these coins,' suggested Jack. 'It looks like there's a path through there – it'll keep us away from the crowd.' He indicated a gap between two houses at the end of the square.

Emmie got up, holding a hand out to her friend. It probably was a good idea to stay away from whatever was happening out on the road for a while at least. They walked through the square and down the narrow pathway at the end, finding that it led out onto a wider street with houses on one side and open ground on the other. 'This is very much the edge of town still, isn't it? Lots more green space than in our time.'

'Yep. Doesn't really feel like London at all when you look in this direction,' he agreed. The dark, sooty air in the distance behind them felt half a world away from this suburban scene. 'Look,' Jack pointed at an apple tree with juicy-looking fruit hanging from its branches. As he reached up to the nearest branch, a loud bark behind him made them both jump. He glanced over his shoulder and saw a large black dog approaching them with a snarl on its face. 'Err—'

'Run!' shouted Emmie, deciding that she didn't like the dog's threatening behaviour. They found themselves with the feeling of being chased yet again and took off down the road as fast as they could. Reaching the end, and doubling over with breathlessness, Jack twisted to see whether the dog was still in pursuit.

'It's... ok...' he panted. 'I think... it's given up...'

There was no reply from Emmie and, when Jack straightened up, he saw his friend staring ahead in stunned silence. Following her gaze, he looked across the wide road in front of them and saw an enormous glass and iron structure glinting in the late afternoon sunlight. It was several stories high in the middle, with an arched roof running across the width. The building entirely filled their view, stretching far outside their peripheral vision. 'What on earth is that?!' he exclaimed, 'it looks like something from another world...'

The Crystal Palace

'I think it might be the Great Exhibition,' replied Emmie slowly. 'I remember learning it was in something they called the 'Crystal Palace', and that certainly looks like a palace!'

Jack unfolded a sheet of paper and held it out to show her. 'I picked this up in the museum earlier – I think you're right,' he said.

Emmie took the paper and stared at it. It was a leaflet showing some of the exhibits from the Victoria and Albert Museum they had been visiting and had a picture of the Great Exhibition of 1851 on the front.

'Do you reckon that's where we'll find this diamond?' asked Jack hopefully. He wasn't sure about this adventure so far – London seemed smaller and smellier than he'd been expecting.

'I think it might – those exhibits in the museum mostly came from the Great Exhibition, so it makes sense to look there.' The pair crossed the road when there was a gap in the horse transport going past. The traffic here was different – more carriages and definitely no handcart sellers. 'If I'm right, then this is

Hyde Park,' Emmie explained. 'Let's go through that gate and take a look around.' Passing through the large, black wrought iron gates alongside a few other people, Emmie suddenly felt a sense of being part of history, as she had done on their previous adventures. This was, in some ways, just London, but being in the presence of the enormous Crystal Palace had a special aura. When they were on board Titanic, the whole ship felt like a chapter from history, as did experiencing an air raid in the Blitz. She felt goosebumps on her arms and shivered a little in anticipation.

'What's up?' asked Jack, noticing her go quiet. 'You're not chickening out, are you?'

'No, it's not that.' She wasn't sure how to explain it to him in a way which didn't sound silly. 'Come on – let's get closer.'

As they walked across the expanse of grass towards the gigantic structure, it became obvious that it wasn't open to the public yet. There were stacks of wooden packing crates lined up outside the entrances, and a constant stream of carts brought more items. They could see through the panes of glass that there were large trees planted inside the exhibition space, and flags of all colours fluttered along the roofline.

'We ain't got time for sightseers – make yourselves useful or get out of here!' A brusque shout jerked Emmie and Jack from their wonderment, and they turned to face the man approaching them. He wore a brown waistcoat over a shirt with rolled up sleeves, and there was a cloth cap jammed on top of his head. 'Well? Are you here for work or not?' he demanded, looking impatient.

Jack glanced at Emmie – this could be a good opportunity to have a look inside. She nodded back at him. 'Ok, what do you need us to do?'

'Come with me then,' the man said, turning to retrace his steps. 'Don't take all day!' he called back over his shoulder.

Following him, Jack and Emmie approached one of the huge glass doors of the pavilion. It stood wide open, held in place by a hook against an ornately carved wooden post. Entering the giant space, which resembled a huge greenhouse, Jack stopped to look up and let out a low whistle. 'It's huge! It must have taken ages to—'

'Like I said – no time for sightseeing,' barked the man. 'See those crates – there's a hundred sets of red drapes inside. Each exhibition stand needs one by tonight – I'd get started if I were you. There's sixpence each if you finish on time.'

Jack lifted the lid on the first crate as the man disappeared. Inside, exactly as he'd said, were layers and layers of folded red cloth. 'Come on,' he said quietly, 'guess we'd better get on with it.'

For the next few hours, the pair walked up and down the immense building, delivering the drapes to each stand, one by one. The Exhibition was obviously almost ready to open, and these decorating tasks were some of the final touches. More than half of the exhibition space seemed relate to British goods and inventions, with other countries having less elaborate stands at one end of the great structure. There was no obvious sight of the diamond though.

'There's certainly a lot of homegrown pride going on, isn't there?' remarked Emmie. 'It feels like we're trying to tell the rest of the world that we're better than them...'

'Yes, it does a bit,' agreed Jack. 'Come on – we've got the stands upstairs to do still before it gets dark.'

*

Eventually, the friends finished and returned to the now-empty crates, unsure what they should do next. It was as if the man had been watching out for them though, as he now appeared from behind a large palm tree.

'Did you finish?' he asked, his tone slightly softer than earlier.

'Yes, all done,' confirmed Emmie, pointing to the empty crates. The man looked around – the stands nearest to them had their drapes arranged decoratively. He nodded and put a hand inside his waistcoat pocket.

'There you go – sixpence each, as promised.'

'Thank you,' they both said, smiling gratefully.

'Now get out of here – it's the big day tomorrow.' Jack and Emmie were both tempted to ask what that meant, but despite the man's softer tone he still didn't seem exactly friendly.

Emmie led the way out of the great glasshouse, gazing around her as they went. It was so big – she wondered how it had all been put together. In some ways, like a giant Meccano set, it was probably made in pieces and then bolted together from a kit. As they passed through the giant doors, she turned to Jack. 'We need to work out how to get back inside, but I can't see that happening until tomorrow now. Shall we find something to eat?'

'Thought you'd never ask!' he grinned back at her. 'I'm starving after all that work.'

Emerging into the twilight of a late spring evening, Emmie pointed back to the park gates. 'We'll have to head into town and see what's open, I guess.' Turning left, knowing they were heading in the direction of Hyde Park Corner, Emmie began to wonder how different the parts of London she knew might be in Victorian times.

As they approached the junction itself, seeing Green Park emerging to their right, Emmie breathed a small sigh of relief. There were a large number of street vendors like they'd seen earlier, with carts set up across the road from the park entrance, and a modest crowd of people surrounding them.

'Mmm, what's that smell?' remarked Jack, sniffing the air. 'I'm hoping it's my tea!' Led by his stomach, he encouraged Emmie across the road, dodging the ever-present piles of horse manure. Approaching one cart with a striped cloth draped over it, he stopped and nudged Emmie. 'Look – pies.'

'Go on then,' agreed Emmie, realising that she was really hungry too.

Jack picked out two pies and handed over the four pence asked by the vendor. As he glanced down at the remaining coins in his hand, he felt a stab of worry over how long they were going to last. The smell of warm pastry wafting up to his nose put that thought aside almost immediately though and he handed a pie to Emmie.

'Thanks,' she said hungrily, taking a bite out of the crust.

'That's good,' mumbled Jack through a mouthful of food. After a moment more chewing, he looked at Emmie and stopped. 'What do you think is in here?'

'I was wondering that too,' she replied, 'it's quite slimy, whatever it is.'

Looking back at the cart, they noticed the seller picking up his sign which had fallen over. In handwritten chalk it read – Eel Pies. 'Urgh,' Jack gagged, 'I wish we'd seen that.' He peered at the remainder of the pie in his hand, suddenly not hungry.

'Scrape the filling out?' suggested Emmie sensibly. 'We don't know what else there's going to be.'

Wandering further along the road as they ate the more palatable parts of their pies, Jack and Emmie's thoughts turned to where they might spend the night, before trying to get back into the pavilion the next day. 'Do you think we might find a room to rent somewhere?' asked Jack. 'I don't expect Victorian London is that safe at night.'

'We'll probably be better off looking along some of these side streets.' Emmie could tell that they needed a less popular location which they could afford with the few pennies they had left. She pointed along a narrow road, with tall buildings leaning in from either side. The street itself was cobbled, and the immediate benefit was a lack of horse droppings, as it appeared too narrow for carts or carriages to use.

Gingerly entering the street, they saw a few of the buildings had signs outside advertising rooms. 'Which one should we try?' Jack asked.

'The first one? We won't know what they're like until we look inside.'

Jack took a step inside the doorway of a house on their left. It smelled of tobacco smoke and unwashed bodies. In the corridor, a small coal stove burned, contributing to the overall aroma. 'Hello?' he said nervously, 'is anyone about?' There was no reply, except a creaking sound from the floorboards above. He looked back at Emmie, who smiled encouragingly at him.

'Try that one,' she said, indicating a door partially shadowed at the end of the corridor.

Jack approached it and knocked on the wooden panel. Silence. He tried again, louder this time. Still nothing. Finally, in desperation, he tried the handle and the door creaked open. He stepped back involuntarily as the smell of stale cooking met his nostrils, then steadied himself and peered through the open door. He took a tentative step into the room, immediately being met with a croaky shout from further inside.

'What d'ya want?!'

'Err. We're looking for a room,' Jack said quietly, wishing this wasn't happening.

'No – we're full. Go away.'

'Is there anywhere—'

'I said go away,' the voice shouted. There was a flurry of movement from inside the room and Jack turned to run, grabbing at Emmie's arm.

'Come on!' he urged, pulling her along the corridor and back out into the street, the door slamming behind them. They ran back to the main road and then paused to catch their breath, chests heaving. 'Oh great...' he muttered, 'now it's raining too...'

A Wet Night

They huddled together in a doorway, looking out at the wet street and trying to make sense of what to do next. Neither of them really wanted to try another house in case they got the same response.

'What do you think?' said Jack quietly.

Emmie glanced around – people were hurrying past, heads down and trying not to get too wet. The street sellers had packed up and the lamplighters were doing their rounds. She watched as one man leaned his ladder up against a nearby lamp post, using the little horizonal bar sticking out to stop the ladder slipping. He climbed up, opened the lamp and lit it, leaning back slightly as the flame popped into life. Immediately, Emmie felt better – there was something about the yellow glow which warmed her, even though she was too far away to feel any heat from it.

Being able to see the railings of Hyde Park opposite now, thanks to the recent illumination, gave her an idea. She turned to Jack with an encouraging smile. 'Shall we see if we can get back into the pavilion somehow? At least it will be dry.'

He nodded in reply. 'Better than getting soaked out here, for sure.' The horse-drawn traffic had largely stopped now, so crossing the road was easier, though avoiding stepping in something unpleasant was still a problem. They ran quickly along the pavement to the grand archway entrance to the park, coming to a halt under the central arch as they realised that the gates were shut. Jack rattled the heavy ironwork, but it was firmly locked. 'What about the gate we used earlier?' he suggested, 'it's not that far.'

Emmie looked out at the rain swirling in the lamplight – they had to do something, but getting any wetter wasn't that appealing. Her brow furrowed for a moment, then cleared as she made up her mind. 'Ok, but only if we run.'

'You got it,' Jack grinned at her. He was quite happy running about all day if needed. 'Ready? One, two, three – go!' They ran along the flagstone pavement, holding hands and laughing manically. There were few people about now – the rain having driven most of them away – but one old man shuffling towards them lifted his head in surprise as the pair sprinted past.

They splashed to a stop outside the entrance from earlier, fairly soaked now and really needing to find some shelter. The gate itself was in shadow – the nearest lamp post being too far away to cast any light over it. Emmie slowly walked forward, feeling for the gate which she knew should be in front of her. 'Oof!'

she exclaimed, stumbling over something on the ground. There was some sudden movement near her feet and, as she fought to retain her balance, something or someone got up and scurried away from the pair. She grabbed onto Jack gratefully. 'What was that?!' she whispered.

'I think it might have been someone sleeping out here,' he whispered back. 'I can think of better places...'

Emmie reached out ahead of her again and touched the cold iron of the gate. It seemed to be across her path, and she slowly felt along it to check. Once she had confirmed that their path was again blocked, she shoved the gate in a rare display of frustration.

'That's not going to help, is it?' observed Jack. His friend was normally so rational, and he didn't like to see her like this. 'If we can't get through it, we're just going to have to go over it.'

'What do you mean?' hissed Emmie, 'the top is spiked.' Indeed, just visible in the dim light, they could see a row of pointed ironwork running along above their heads.

'Not the gate,' Jack replied, 'we'll go over the wall.'

Emmie stared up at the stone structure – she could just about see the top, and there wasn't much in the way of hand holds. Squinting again, she noticed a thin lip and wondered if they could reach it. 'Give me a leg up?' she asked. They moved out of the shelter of the arch, and Jack bent down to cup his hands for her to put a foot on. He took her weight and stood up, leaning against the stonework as the rain continued to fall.

'Can you reach it?' he grunted, struggling to get her any higher up. There was a similar grunt from Emmie, and he could feel her stretching for the lip.

'Got it!' she said triumphantly, and he felt a bit of her weight shift as she tried to pull herself up. One last heave of effort and she disappeared onto the top of the wall, legs flailing and almost kicking him in the face.

'Oi! Watch it,' he muttered, only half-joking. They'd solved part of the problem of getting into the park – now how was he going to get over?

Emmie lay on the wall and dangled her arms down to Jack. He held on and tried to lift himself high enough to reach the lip, but it was no good – he needed something to stand on. Feeling dejected, he looked back the way they'd come and noticed a large tree branch hanging over the wall near the next lamp post. It was too high still but had given him an idea.

'Can you walk along the wall to that branch?' he called up to Emmie. 'If you climb on it, then it might droop enough for me to reach it at the end. Emmie crouched and slowly made her way to the branch, taking care not to slip off in the rain. She sat astride it and lifted up her legs to use as much weight as possible.

Jack looked up at the branch – it was definitely lower, but still a way above his head. 'Can you shuffle down a bit?' he suggested, watching Emmie tentatively moving. The branch moved a little further this time and Jack jumped for it. He grabbed on with both hands – this was the easy part though. Now he needed his best pull-up effort to try and get on properly. Straining, he hauled himself up, getting his chin level with the branch before his arms gave out. Sensing his frustration, Emmie tried to move forwards again and had to ease herself around a small upright branch.

'Try again?' she suggested through gritted teeth. It wasn't any fun at all trying to hold onto a slippery tree in the pouring rain. Jack peered upwards and jumped again – Emmie's last effort had made the difference, and he slowly pulled himself up so he could swing a leg over the branch.

Exhaling in relief, he smiled in Emmie's direction and they both shuffled back to the wall. Dropping down into the park, he looked around for some shelter. There was some light from the lamp post on the other side of the wall shining in a narrow arc, but most of their surroundings were in darkness. There was a large bush close to them, and Jack guided Emmie to it – hoping for partial respite from the rain at least.

'This isn't much better, is it?' said Emmie quietly, as they crouched underneath the foliage. 'I'm soaked and cold.'

Jack thought for a moment. 'Remember all those packing cases outside the pavilion? There was a tarpaulin over some of them – we might be able to shelter under that.' Without waiting for a reply, he grabbed her hand and started walking quickly towards the pavilion entrance. Everything appeared entirely different at night – a lot less impressive when you couldn't see the full scale of the exhibition hall – though the pair barely noticed as they hunted for cover.

'Over here!' called Emmie, dragging back some heavy sheeting and exposing three empty crates underneath. They weren't very big, but looked dry, and that was good enough. Jack climbed into one and Emmie joined him, pulling back the cover over the top before sitting down.

'Well, this is fun,' began Jack. 'At least I had a cabin on Titanic...'

Emmie was silent. She didn't quite know what to say to him – they'd both agreed to go on this latest adventure, but it wasn't shaping up quite as well as their previous ones. They knew what they had to do, but not how to do it, and life in Victorian London was definitely hard.

'How do you feel about sleeping outside really?' Jack continued, trying to get some kind of response from his friend. 'It feels a bit odd, doesn't it. Creepy even.'

'Not scared, are you?' retorted Emmie.

'No, not exactly. I think as long as we're together it'll be all right,' he said gently, realising that solving this mystery would need both of their efforts. 'I guess we need to find a pawn shop tomorrow and try to get some more money though. It's hard to tell how long we'll be stuck here for.'

'And then we need to get back into the pavilion.' Emmie was convinced that was the most sensible place to look for the diamond, and it felt like the sooner they got home this time the better.

Warming Up

Emmie was dreaming. She was in a boat during a storm and was being tossed about by the waves. They'd soaked her – crashing over the boat and threatening to capsize it. The more waves that hit the boat, the more it rocked around. It was going to tip over. No, it wasn't. Yes, it was...

THUMP!

She woke with a start, finding herself in a crumpled damp heap, head lying on Jack's leg. Then the boat moved again. Except it wasn't a boat, was it? They were still in the packing case they'd crawled into last night to escape the rain – only now it was being moved. She pulled at the corner of the tarpaulin, seeing a sliver of sky bouncing around outside. Nudging Jack, she peeled it back further and cautiously peered out. The packing case was still moving, and it wasn't on the ground. Perplexed, she gave Jack another push to wake him up. 'Oi!' she hissed in his direction.

'W-what's the matter?' he said groggily, opening one eye.

'We're moving – have a look.' With that, Emmie popped her head up out of the crate and then ducked down again just as quickly. 'Umm – it looks like we're on some sort of cart,' she said, hardly believing it herself. 'They must be clearing up and have moved the crate.'

'Don't be daft,' Jack retorted, rubbing his eyes. 'Let me see.' Before he had a chance to look, any doubt was extinguished as they both heard a loud whinny from just ahead of the crate.

'And there's the horse!' exclaimed Emmie. 'What are we going to do?'

'Get out of here before we find ourselves somewhere we don't want to be,' suggested Jack. He looked over the top of the crate now – seeing that they were heading out of the park by the same gate they'd tried in vain to get through last night. 'Come on,' he said, swinging a leg over the side, 'we need to go before this thing gets onto the road.'

They both dropped the metre or so from the cart's load bed and tried to casually walk away. It was almost a success – they'd got a few paces towards the gate when there was a shout from behind them. Emmie stopped, holding onto Jack's hand – did they run or hold their nerve?

'You look frozen. Come over here.' The pair turned and saw a group of workmen gathered around a brazier. The fire looked warm and inviting on the cool spring morning, and Jack shivered in his still damp clothes.

'Let's warm up a little,' he said. 'Just for a while.'

Emmie frowned – wondering why the man was being so helpful. Did he want something from them? 'Are you sure?' she whispered to Jack.

Seeing their indecision, the man spoke again. 'It's alright – us less fortunate ones need to stick together, don't we?'

'Please,' said Jack quietly, shivering again and causing Emmie to drop her shoulders in resignation.

They approached the man who had called out – he had a red face and big fluffy sideburns escaping from under his cap. He seemed friendly enough, so hopefully it would be ok.

'Bit wet, aren't you?' the man asked. 'You must have been out all night.'

Jack nodded. 'Couldn't find anywhere to sleep. Everywhere seemed full.'

'Well,' the man replied, 'if you're sticking around, try Chandler Street – there's a few lodging houses down there which the workers here have been using. As this is all built now, there'll likely be some space.'

'Thanks,' Jack said, rubbing his hands together near the fire and thinking how much more friendly people were than in modern London. He was trying to stand as close as possible so that his clothes would begin to dry – the shirt and waistcoat were still soaked, and his trousers were quite wet too.

Emmie looked down at her arms which were trembling. The man noticed this too. 'Come closer, miss, warm yourself' he said gently. 'Tobias, hand me that pan and some water,' he instructed, turning to an older boy beside him. He balanced it on the edge of the brazier and stood back. 'We were about done breakfasting, but I'll get something warm for you to take the chill off.' When the water had boiled, he bent down and poured it into a container at his feet. A moment later he stood up and handed a small mug to each of them.

'Thank you so much.' Emmie was grateful for the chance to hold something warm, let alone drink it. When she did, she tasted weak tea – they must have re-used some leaves – but it felt like the best drink she'd ever had. Slightly warmer now, she wondered if this man could give them any useful information. 'What's going on here today?' she asked.

'Ah, well – that's a thing,' replied the man. 'You see – we've finished building and filling this great space, and now we're no longer required. We've got to be out of here this morning before the grand opening later on.'

'Where will you go?' asked Jack.

'You know – here and there,' replied the man. 'We'll find work somewhere else in this fine city, I'm sure of it. Anyway, you two look a bit warmer now and we must be off. Good luck - say hello to the Queen for me if you see her.' With that, he beckoned to the rest of the workers, and they slowly ambled off towards the park gates.

Emmie turned to Jack; her face flushed in excitement. 'What was that about the Queen, do you think?' She wondered if it was possible that Queen Victoria herself would be coming to the grand opening.

'I reckon she'll be opening it in person,' Jack said, earning a small shriek of excitement from Emmie. 'Better than that – it'll be a great time to look around inside whilst everyone else is distracted by the opening ceremony.' He turned round to warm the back of his clothes against the fire. It wasn't as hot now – the wood the workers had fed it having almost burned through. 'I think we should see about some breakfast, and also try to find a pawn shop. We can head back here this afternoon for the opening.'

*

And so they found themselves walking back towards Hyde Park Corner – this time not having to worry about puddles, gates and rain. The sun was coming out from behind a cloud and drying up all evidence of last night's downpour. Emmie adjusted her skirt – it was almost dry now, and her hands no longer felt cold for the first time since yesterday evening. 'Let's go this way,' she suggested, steering them down Grosvenor Place and behind the Buckingham Palace gardens.

The roads were busy again with traffic – the same mix of omnibuses and carts being pulled along as they'd seen the day before. There was something in the air too – maybe a sense of excitement at the prospect of the Great Exhibition opening later that day. People seemed to be smiling and chatting more today, and there was less impatience from the different groups of road users.

Reaching the end of the road, Jack noticed a bakery with a small queue outside. 'Breakfast time!' he announced, joining the queue and pressing his face up against the glass to see what treats lay inside. 'Pie or bread,' he said, pulling his face away and leaving a steamed-up circle on the window pane.

'Bread, I think,' replied Emmie, having not really got over the eel pie from yesterday. 'I'd like to enjoy my breakfast...' Jack reached the front of the queue and slipped into the shop, returning with a small loaf of wholemeal bread.

'This is it, I'm afraid. Our remaining eight pence doesn't buy much.' He tore the bread in half and passed a piece to Emmie, who took a hungry bite.

'Mmm,' she said through a mouthful, 'tastes alright.' They carried on walking as they ate and stumbled across a drinking fountain set against some railings. 'Do you think it's safe to drink?' Emmie wondered aloud, remembering some of the nasty diseases she had learned about in school.

'Course it is, miss. I stop here every day on my way to work,' came a voice from behind them. A young girl, not much older than they were, stepped past and took a long drink from the fountain. 'See? I'm ok,' she said with a grin, before carrying on down the pavement.

Emmie bent down to the fountain and pressed the metal lever to make the water flow. It gurgled and then splashed into the basin in front of her. She put her head to the stream and took a drink. 'She's right – it's good,' confirmed Emmie, standing aside to let Jack have a turn too.

Suddenly, she ran off down the pavement. Jack stared after her – what was she doing? Should he stay or follow her? As he watched, she caught up with the girl who had spoken to them, exchanged a few words and then headed back towards him.

'Guess what?' she said, with a grin. 'There's a pawn shop down the road.' Jack felt a sense of relief flow through him – pawning his coins was their best chance of obtaining some money to survive on. There was no telling how long it would take to find out what had happened to the diamond, and he was still hungry.

The Pawn Shop

The pawn shop looked slightly tired. The black paint around the door was peeling and the big front window needed a wash. The sign Jack had described was hanging above the door – 3 slightly tarnished, golden-coloured balls on a bracket which wasn't quite straight.

'Looks a bit...' Emmie wasn't sure quite which adjective best described the sight in front of her.

'We just need it to be open,' Jack said. 'Try to look past the decoration. Or lack of it.' He reached for the door and gave it a push. It opened slowly, with a moderate amount of creaking, revealing a dim interior. Jack glanced back at Emmie, who nodded encouragingly.

'We need to get some money. I've got a feeling once that's sorted it'll feel a lot better,' she said.

Hesitantly, Jack stepped inside the shop, with Emmie close behind. The interior was more battered than outside, if that were possible. Glass-fronted cabinets lined the walls, containing row upon row of pawned objects. At the end of the shop a metal grille covered the counter, with a small slot set in front of the man who stood behind it. He scratched his bald head and stared at Jack as he approached, studying this strange-looking boy who seemed better dressed and fed than his usual customers.

'How can I help you?' the man said, never taking his eyes off Jack. Emmie noticed that there were mirrors positioned in several of the corners of the shop – presumably to help the man see what customers were up to without coming out from behind his counter.

'Erm,' started Jack, reaching into his pocket for the coins and bringing them out into the light. He saw the man's eyes glint at the sight of the money – he was obviously interested. 'I'd like to know how much these are worth, please,' he asked.

'Hand them over then,' replied the man, a little too eagerly for Jack's liking. He hesitated for a moment, weighing the two coins in his hand and feeling slightly uneasy. Should he give them to the man or not?

'Go on,' he heard Emmie say quietly behind him, and stepped forward with the coins. Placing them on the counter, next to the hole in the grille, Jack stepped back and waited to see what happened next.

The man picked up one of the coins, turned it over in his hand, and looked curiously at the pair. 'Where are these from then?'

Jack hadn't been expecting the question and thought quickly. 'Not sure. We found them.'

'Did you now...?' Jack didn't like the man's tone and was beginning to regret coming into the shop at all. 'Wait here a minute,' he said, before turning and leaving them alone in the shop.

'Shall we get out of here?' Jack was really unsure about this now. He'd thought that somehow the modern coins would just be treated as something foreign, and they'd be able to get some money for them. The man seemed to be suspicious – or maybe he'd just run off with the coins?

'Give him a bit longer – maybe he's gone to look up how much they're worth, or weigh them?' Emmie suggested. She thought it was odd that he had disappeared too.

Minutes passed, and there was still no sign of the man. It was eerily quiet in the shop, especially since the pavement outside had been quite busy. Jack tapped his foot impatiently. 'I've got a bad feeling about this,' he insisted.

'I think you might be right,' conceded Emmie. 'I don't think he's coming back.' Maybe the man had run off with their coins after all. She wondered how they were going to eat later, with the few pennies from their work the previous day having already been spent. At that moment, Jack's stomach rumbled as if to agree with her. 'Come on – there's no point in hanging around here all day,' she sighed. Turning to the door, Emmie gave the handle a tug. As it swung reluctantly open, she blinked in the sunlight which streamed in. A few minutes in the gloom of the shop's interior and her eyes needed to re-adjust.

Stepping out onto the pavement, they paused momentarily to discuss what to do next. There were still a lot of people walking past and, as Emmie turned back the way they'd come, a shout came from further down the street. 'Stop! You – stop now!'

Thinking it was the man from the shop returning at last, Jack and Emmie looked in the direction of the voice. 'Oh – it's just a policeman,' said Jack disappointedly.

The policeman shouted again and blew a whistle loudly. He was running down the pavement in their direction, and just behind him came the man from the pawn shop.

Confused, Jack stared at the onrushing policeman and wondered why the shopkeeper was following him. 'Oh no...' said Emmie – catching on quicker than he had.

'You two need to come with me,' announced the policeman as he stopped beside them, red-faced and slightly out of breath.

'W-why?' stammered Jack. 'What have we done?' His knees felt weak as his brain started to make sense of the scene in front of him.

'We need to talk about these,' he said sternly, opening his hand to reveal the coins Jack had tried to pawn. 'You'll be coming to the station to explain yourselves.' Jack tried to say something, but the words wouldn't come out, whilst Emmie stared open-mouthed over the policeman's shoulder. Picking its way through the traffic was a black wagon with barred windows, pulled by two chestnut horses. It pulled up alongside them and another policeman jumped down.

'King Street?' he asked. The first policeman nodded.

'Forgery, and possibly theft too,' he said. 'You'll need to take these coins – they're evidence.'

Jack felt sick – what had he got them into? He tried to protest, but the second policeman waved his words away, put a firm hand on his shoulder and marched he and Emmie to the back of the wagon. He took a bunch of keys from his belt and opened the door at the rear. Giving them a little shove in the right direction, the policeman steered the pair up a step and inside, slamming the door after them.

Emmie looked at Jack, then around the inside of their prison. It was dirty, worn and smelled of stale sweat. There were a number of stains on the walls and floor, and she didn't really want to think about where they might have come from. As she stared, Emmie noticed the graffiti which was carved into the walls and bench, then stopped as she thought about the people who had written it. The reality hit her at that point – they were in a police van, accused of a crime, and somewhere they weren't really meant to be. How were they even going to give their details at the station? Neither of the houses they lived in had been built in 1951, let alone 1851... For a moment, she didn't know what to say, then her annoyance spilled over. 'Why did you have to suggest pawning those coins?' she demanded. 'What if they put us in prison – how will we ever get home again then?' Her mind whirled – no diamond would mean no coronation... It was all on them to solve this problem, and now they didn't even have their freedom.

Jack sniffed quietly to himself opposite her. She looked across at her friend again and saw that he was close to tears. He knew his idea had gone badly wrong and didn't need her judgement too. 'Are you ok?' she asked quietly.

He nodded, swallowing as his eyes welled up. 'Uh-huh.'

'It'll be ok – they'll realise it's a misunderstanding when we get to the police station.' Emmie felt guilty at being cross with Jack and was now trying to sound more confident than she felt.

With a jerk, the wagon moved off, bumping along the cobbled street. Emmie could see out of the small, barred window and realised they were heading back towards Hyde Park Corner. She stared at the other carriages and carts on the road and wished they were on any one of them, rather than stuck in here.

A few minutes later, Jack looked up. 'We're in big trouble, aren't we? Do you really think they might put us in prison?' he asked quietly. 'I wish we'd never come on this school trip—'

Whatever else Jack might have said was abruptly drowned out by the noise of their arrival at the police station. There was a lot of shouting, and someone banged hard on the side of the wagon. 'Stand clear!'

Jack and Emmie stood up, backing away from the door just as the policeman who had locked them in appeared at the window. He peered in, satisfied that they weren't about to rush him, and unlocked the door. As it opened, Emmie saw a crowd of people standing in front of a grey building. There was a large lamp over the door and a sign which read 'Police'.

The crowd murmured as they were led out into the daylight and across to the police station. Several people pointed and laughed, before a voice from somewhere in the group rang out. 'They're only kids...'

That's right – thought Emmie. They were only kids, and how were they going to get out of this one...?

Stuck In The Cells

Emmie gazed up at the dirty grey walls of the police station as they were led inside. It looked like an unfriendly place, but she supposed it hadn't been built to look welcoming. As they passed through the doorway, the friends found themselves in a wood-panelled reception area – a large desk running the entire width of the room and, ominously, a heavily barred door to the left. There was a tall policeman behind the desk, wearing glasses and with a large moustache – it was him who they were led over to.

'These two were trying to pass fake coins in a pawn shop,' the policeman who had brought them in said, placing Jack's coins on the counter. The man behind the desk glared at Jack and Emmie, before reaching for a large ledger book.

'Names?' he said, with a higher voice than his size suggested. His pen hovered over the book as he waited.

'Emmie. Emmie Langford.' Her knees shook as she answered the man. She had never been inside a police station before, let alone under arrest.

'And you?' he pointed at Jack. 'Do you have a name too?'

'Jack Bishop,' he said quietly, worried about what was coming next.

'Right – well you can wait in the cells until we've decided what to do with you.' He turned to a hatch behind him and called through it. 'Tyler? Two more for the holding cells.' A moment later, the barred door swung open, and an older policeman appeared.

'Follow me,' he instructed. His face looked kind, though he was still obviously going to lock them up. As the door clanged shut behind them and the man turned a key in the lock, the removal of their liberty felt very real. 'You're in this one,' he said to Jack, opening the door to a large cell and ushering him inside. Emmie followed him further along a passageway, hearing a slurred voice behind her begin to speak to Jack inside the cell. 'And this is you,' he announced – stopping at a dark green door, with a sliding window set in it. He checked inside and then unlocked the door for her. Emmie found her feet unwilling to cross the threshold and felt her heart start to race – this was more trouble than she had ever been in before. She wondered how long she might have to stay in this horrible place.

'Do I have to?' she whispered, looking at the policeman with pleading eyes.

'Afraid so, miss. They're the rules.'

Emmie reluctantly stepped inside the cell, then jumped as the door shut behind her. The sound of the key turning in the lock made her shudder, and she sank down onto a bench in despair. The slurred voice from the next cell was still questioning Jack and, if there was one thing to be grateful for, it was that she was alone – for now at least.

*

After a while, the silence felt deafening. The grey tiled walls and floor were cold, and the small, barred window high up seemed to be taunting her with a glimpse of the sky. The clouds were free – why was she stuck in here? She ran through the earlier events in the pawn shop again and again in her head – should they have done anything differently? There was no ready answer, except that fate had put them here and it seemed unlikely fate was going to get them out again.

Feeling a burst of irritation run through her, Emmie suddenly got to her feet and rushed over to the door, hammering on it with her fists and shouting to be let out. 'We haven't done anything!' she yelled as loudly as she could. No-one came, and in the end she slumped back down on to the bench, defeated.

'Emmie!' called Jack's voice a moment later. 'Are you ok?' There was little else he could do at that moment, especially as it was obvious that she was not all right. 'Try and keep it together,' he added.

Emmie sobbed quietly to herself, trying not to let Jack hear in the next cell. She always felt a responsibility to be the strong one, even when she was struggling herself. One of them had to keep it together, though today she didn't much want it to be her. She curled up on the bench, staring at the floor and trying to pretend to herself that they weren't in this mess. Even the large spider which scuttled across the floor and then into a crack between the tiles seemed to be mocking her with the freedom it enjoyed.

Sometime later, the little window in the door slid open with a bang, surprising her. A face peered in, then the sound of a key rattled in the lock. Emmie sat up expectantly, hoping that this was the moment everyone realised there had been a terrible mistake. The door swung open and there stood a young policeman with a metal tray. He placed it down on the end of the bench silently and then retreated. Emmie's heart sank – she wasn't getting out. If anything, the fact that they were being fed indicated she would be here longer. She stared down at the food – there was a cup of water, a bowl of thin, grey-looking soup, and a chunk of bread. She wasn't hungry anyway, but this was hardly an inspiring meal. Idly, she stirred the soup with the spoon, noticing a film of grease on top and some chunks of something unidentified floating in it. Dropping the spoon back into the metal bowl with a clang, she sat back with her head in her hands.

There was literally nothing to do in that cell apart from be alone with your thoughts. Emmie could easily understand how people might go insane in solitary confinement – it had only been a couple of hours and that was bad enough. She looked at the food again – maybe the bread might be a bit more appetising. Still not hungry, but smart enough to realise she didn't know where her next meal was coming from, she chewed on a corner of the bread. It was ok – a bit dry but edible. Feeling slightly better with some food inside her, she heard footsteps outside the door. She quickly stuffed the rest of the bread into her mouth in the expectation that the tray would shortly be taken away.

Bang! went the flap on the door, followed a moment later by a key turning in the lock. As the door opened, she could see a different policeman outside. 'Come on then. On your feet,' he said.

'What for?' asked Emmie uncertainly. She was expecting the food to be cleared and then left to her thoughts again.

'You're to come with me please. Now.'

This was odd in several ways – not least of all because, now she had a way out of the cell, she wasn't sure whether she wanted to take it or not. However, the policeman left her little choice in the end as he walked into the cell and steered her out through the door. She followed him slowly along the passage and he stopped in front of the cell Jack had been put into. What was going on?

'Finally!' Jack said as the door was opened. 'That bloke's snoring was getting right on my nerves. Where are we going then?'

Emmie shook her head. 'No idea,' she whispered.

'This way then,' ordered the policeman, taking them back the way they had arrived earlier. Emmie's heart fluttered with a small burst of excitement as they approached the door back into the reception area, only to be dashed as they were taken straight past.

'This place is massive inside,' said Jack, seemingly talking to cover his nervousness. Emmie nodded, focused on the man in front and where he was taking them.

Eventually, they came to a heavy door with a brass handle and a little sign on it, which read simply 'Room 3'. The policeman put his hand on the handle and opened the door, ushering them inside. Immediately, a strong metallic smell greeted their nostrils, and they could see four wooden chairs around a central table.

'Sit down,' instructed the policeman, 'he'll be along in a bit.'

'Who's 'he'?' Emmie asked, but was only answered by the sound of the closing door. She looked across at Jack. 'What happened to you in the cell? I heard that man slurring away talking to you.'

'Oh, he was just talking nonsense. I ignored him for a bit and then he fell asleep.' Jack studied her face for a bit. 'Are you ok? You look upset.'

'I... It's just—'

Before Emmie had a chance to answer properly, the door behind them swept open and yet another policeman came in, this time followed by a tall man in a dark suit and overcoat. He was wearing a bowler hat and carried a leather case. The man paused to take off his coat and hat, then turned to them. Emmie's face froze – it was the time architect! What was he doing here...?

Back On Track

'This,' the policeman announced rather pompously, 'is Mr Briggs. He would like a word with you for some reason.'

'Would you mind waiting outside please?' asked the time architect politely. He waited while the policeman thought about refusing, then reluctantly left the room.

'What are you doing here?!' asked Emmie as soon as the door had shut.

The man put a warning finger to his lips. 'Careful – we have to be quiet, so we're not overheard.' He stared at them in turn. 'How are you doing?'

Jack looked at Emmie, who spoke first. 'Well, being stuck in here wasn't our first choice obviously...'

Mr Briggs – if that was his real name – nodded slowly. 'I can sort that out for you,' he said.

Emmie gasped – how could it be that simple?

Jack was going down a different route in his mind though – he stared quizzically at the man. 'If you can travel in time, how come we're finding your diamond? Why don't you just look for it yourself?'

'Jack!' cried Emmie. Being rude to the person who was going to get them released wasn't a clever idea.

'It's ok,' the man said, 'it's a fair question.' He leaned in a bit closer and lowered his voice so that he was almost whispering. 'I can't travel at will – all I can do is help those in difficulties. Once I've got you out, then I'll be gone again.'

'But weren't you there all the time on Titanic?' Emmie was confused by what she was hearing, though reassured that the man would appear if they were ever in real danger.

'Yes – you were in real danger from the moment you stepped onto that ship though. We all know how the story ends.'

Jack looked at the man again. 'So, what happens when we find the diamond?'

'Like I said before – I'll be able to tell you everything then.' The man got to his feet, reaching for his overcoat and hat. 'But now, I've got to get you out. Wait here a moment and I'll sort everything – including retrieving those coins. We can't risk the butterfly effect, can we? Changing anything in history can sometimes have unexpected consequences.'

He left the room, and Jack fixed Emmie with a questioning gaze. 'Do you believe him?' he asked.

'Do you? I don't think we have a choice – he's given us this adventure and now he's helping us when we're stuck. Seems pretty trustworthy to me.'

A few short minutes later and the door opened again. It was the pompous policeman, and this time he was alone. Emmie and Jack exchanged glances – hopefully this was it. 'Follow me, please,' the policeman instructed, walking swiftly back out of the room.

They passed through a couple of green doors, then found themselves outside in a courtyard. To their left, a large pair of wooden gates stood ajar, and across the courtyard the horse-drawn wagon they had arrived in was parked. Emmie swallowed nervously – surely there wasn't a last twist in this episode…

'Through those gates and don't come back!' said the policeman, turning on his heel and going back inside. Jack took Emmie's hand, grinned and pulled her through the opening and back out onto the busy London street. The adventure was definitely back on!

Emmie looked nervously behind them as they passed through the gates, half expecting it to be a trick and for a policeman to come running.

'Let's get out of here,' said Jack, seeing her face and realising that he felt the same. 'We need to keep out of trouble too – I don't fancy ever going back in there.' He guided Emmie along the pavement and across towards Green Park. There were a lot of people about, many dressed elegantly, and it felt like they were all heading to the same place. The flow on the pavement was much heavier in the direction they were walking in.

'Hey – look over there!' said Emmie suddenly. A large crowd were rushing across the park and, as she watched, more people started heading in the same direction. Many were holding their hats or clutching at skirts as they hurried across the grass.

'I wonder what that's all about?' Jack's interest was piqued, and the pair quickened their pace to see what was going on. As they reached the back of the crowd, a cheer went up and Jack could see a fancy carriage sweep past, with mounted horsemen riding alongside. 'Do you think that's the Queen?' he whispered to Emmie.

'She's off to open the Exhibition.' A lady wearing a pink hat beside them had heard Jack's question. 'It'll be a grand ceremony for sure.'

'I'd love to see Queen Victoria in person,' admitted Emmie. 'She always looked so regal.'

'Let's go then,' smiled Jack, 'we were going to search the pavilion again, so we may as well do both at the same time.' He pointed in the direction of Hyde Park. 'It's going to be busy though, looks like everyone else has had the same idea...' Most of the crowd had begun to follow in the direction of the carriage, presumably so they could see more of the royal party too.

They quickly walked over to Hyde Park Corner and crossed the road. The gates to the park were open, but their way was blocked by street vendors selling all kinds of souvenirs. There were postcards, embroidered handkerchiefs and, to Emmie's disappointment, the pie stall from the day before. Grabbing Jack's hand and dodging between the people clustered around the carts, they managed to get into the park. There was a long queue stretching into the distance, people clutching paper tickets and talking excitedly.

'Come on – let's go around the other side and see if we can see the Queen arrive,' suggested Jack. 'I don't want to spend all afternoon in that queue.' He led them along the side of the Serpentine, looping back towards the grand front entrance of the pavilion. There was a big crowd here too, arranged in a semi-circle around the entrance as if they were waiting for someone.

'I don't think she's here yet,' said Emmie excitedly. 'Can we stay and wait?'

'Sure,' replied Jack, 'we'll get a good view from here.' Reluctant to get too close to the entrance, the pair found themselves on slightly higher ground, giving them a good panorama of events. 'Isn't it odd to see the sky without any planes in it?' Jack said. 'You don't really notice them until they aren't there.'

After a few minutes, the noise of the crowd rose excitedly, and Jack could see people turning to look at the park gates. The top of a carriage came into view over the wall, then a pair of soldiers on horseback entered the park. As he watched, the riders were followed by the same carriage they had seen a few minutes earlier, and a further pair of horsemen. The procession swept through the entrance and came to a halt in front of the great glass building. The excited chatter around them continued as a coachman dismounted and opened the carriage door. A tall man stepped out, dressed in black trousers and a red tunic. He had a blue sash over one shoulder, and a sword at his side. The crowd began to clap, as the man turned and offered his hand to a woman still inside the carriage. As she emerged, there were shouts of 'God save the Queen!' and 'Rule Britannia!' She turned, resplendent in a white dress with pink skirts and accompanying blue sash and waved at the crowd. The clapping turned to cheering, and then another figure stepped out of the carriage. The crowd fell silent as a young girl, maybe eight years old, joined the Queen and her husband. She was dressed elegantly in a long white gown and walked alongside the royal couple.

'Why has everyone gone quiet?' whispered Jack. 'Who is the little girl anyway?'

'I can't imagine that most of them have seen anyone with black skin before,' replied Emmie. She was right – there was no malice in the crowd's behaviour, just intrigue.

A courtier appeared, formally announcing the royal arrival. 'Ladies and gentlemen – the Queen, the Prince Consort and Princess Sarah.' A bugle sounded, and the Queen passed through into the exhibition space, the four guardsmen and the rest of the crowd following at a respectful distance.

'Princess Sarah?' mused Emmie, 'I've never heard of her before. I knew Queen Victoria had children, but I imagine she's not one of them.' She felt uncomfortable at what had happened when Sarah had stepped down from the carriage. To her and Jack, people were equal – skin colour, like many things, didn't matter. She understood that, in 1851, London was anything but diverse, but it still didn't feel right to react differently to someone based on their appearance.

Jack looked at the crowd of people streaming into the pavilion. 'Let's go in – maybe we can look about whilst everyone's distracted?' Emmie nodded, and he led the way towards the great doors.

'Ticket?' asked a smartly suited man at the entrance, holding out a gloved hand. Emmie glanced at Jack, who shrugged. 'No ticket, no entry,' the man said, turning to the people behind them. 'Off you go,' he muttered over his shoulder, seeing that they were still standing there.

Jack stepped to the side, feeling despondent again. How were they going to get in without a ticket, or the money to buy one?

The Grand Opening

Emmie led Jack away from the door and sat down on the grass, motioning him to sit alongside her. 'We need a plan,' she said, 'something a bit creative that'll get us inside.'

Jack gazed around – the glass walls seemed far too high to consider climbing up to one of the roof vents, and the crowd of people at the front door showed no sign of dissipating. He scratched his head, and a thoughtful expression came over his face. 'What about—'

TAP! TAP! They both jumped at the noise coming from directly behind them. Turning to look, they saw a boy the other side of the glass, half-hidden between the plants which lined the windows. He had a big grin and was waving to them. Jack half-heartedly waved back, then focused on Emmie again. Before he could speak, the boy had knocked on the window once more and was gesturing towards the corner of the pavilion.

'He seems to want us to look at something,' said Jack. Emmie shrugged in reply and stood up – there was no harm in looking, surely. They walked alongside the boy, who ducked in and out of the foliage on his side of the window as he went. He seemed to be dressed smartly in a shirt and trousers, as if he were either a visitor or had a job inside. Reaching the corner, Jack saw that a door was set into one of the glass frames, and watched as the boy turned a handle which was only on the inside, easing it open. He looked at Emmie in excitement – maybe this was the piece of luck they needed?

'Want to come in?' the boy asked. He held the door a little wider for them, looking very pleased with himself. 'It's ok – they only check tickets on the door. Once you're in, you're in.' Jack and Emmie stepped inside, immediately noticing the chatter of background noise from the visitors. It was much louder than the previous afternoon when the workers were rushing to complete the set up.

'Thanks mate,' Jack said, smiling back at the boy. 'How did you know we wanted to come in?'

'I was watching when you got turned away,' he replied. 'Anyway, everyone wants to come in, so it was an easy guess.' He paused briefly, staring unashamedly at them both. 'Are you here to look around, or do you want to have some fun?' He was a bit bored and liked the idea of people his own age to spend some time with.

Jack was about to reply, but Emmie beat him to it. 'What kind of fun were you thinking of?' It might be useful to have a friend who knew their way around inside the pavilion.

'Well – the Queen's about to perform the opening ceremony, and I know how to get a great view,' he said proudly. 'I'm Albert, by the way – people call me Bert. I'm named after the Prince.'

'I'm Emmie, and this is Jack,' she said. 'We'd love to see the Queen if you can show us.'

'Follow me then!' Bert pulled a curtain back and disappeared behind it. Emmie looked at Jack for a moment, then ducked behind the curtain too, holding it for him to follow.

*

The space they were in was dark and cramped. It smelled stuffy, and Emmie could feel her shoulders brushing the walls on either side. They were following Bert, mostly by touch, and he had warned them in a whispered voice not to make too much noise. Every so often, a slant of light punctured the darkness, and Emmie could see out into the main hall. They seemed to be in a passage which ran between the exhibition stands along one side of the giant pavilion. As they passed each stand, she could hear many different voices – both of visitors and the exhibitors themselves.

'Oi!' Jack hissed, as she stumbled into him in the dark.

'Shh!' came Bert's voice from ahead of them. 'We need to keep really quiet here.' It became obvious why a moment later, as the passage widened slightly, and Bert guided them forward alongside him. 'Ready?' he whispered, before slowly easing the curtain in front of them to one side.

Emmie put a hand to her mouth in a mixture of shock and awe. They were looking out at a huge tree right in the middle of the pavilion. Ahead the tree stood a raised dais, and the royal party were just stepping up onto it, flanked by their red-uniformed guards – Prince Albert following a pace behind the Queen. She had a momentary flash of panic – surely with so many people around, someone would see them?

As if reading her mind, Bert leaned over and whispered in her ear. 'They're all looking at the Queen – they'll never notice us.' She smiled and stepped aside slightly so that Jack could see properly too.

'Wow!' he breathed. This was surely better than all of their previous adventures put together. History could seem boring sometimes, but seeing a figure like Queen Victoria brought to life was incredible.

The Queen stepped up to a lectern and the crowd fell silent. She looked around for a moment, surveying the packed room, and then began to speak. 'It is my very deep pleasure,' she paused for effect, 'to stand here before you all and declare this Great Exhibition open.' A pair of scissors were produced, and she stepped forward to cut a crimson ribbon which spanned the width of the room in front of the dais. The crowd clapped, politely at first – then rising in a crescendo as they showed their appreciation. Queen Victoria smiled benevolently, pausing briefly to give the official artist a chance to capture the scene in his sketch pad, ready to work on a portrait later. She then stepped down, ready to be shown around the exhibition space.

Emmie realised that she had been holding her breath throughout most of this – so enthralled was she, and also terrified that someone would notice them. She slowly let the curtain drop and turned to face Bert. 'That was amazing,' she said. 'I've always wanted to see the Queen. I'm so glad you shared it with us – thank you.'

Bert may have blushed at this point, but it was too dark for anyone to be certain. 'That's ok,' he said shyly.

'How did you know about this place? You seemed to know just where to go,' Jack joined in.

'That's easy – they've been practising for days,' explained Bert. 'My parents both have jobs here – Mother sells cigarettes and Father is one of the foremen – helping build the stands and keeping everything running. I just hang around in case anyone needs me to do anything.' He looked around the space they were in and gestured with his arm. 'This was built on purpose to allow stands to be stocked up without the public seeing.'

'So, can you walk around the whole building without being seen?' asked Emmie. She was beginning to think of how this could be really useful.

'Yep,' confirmed Bert, 'where do you want to go?'

'Are there any displays of precious stones – you know, diamonds and things?'

'They're near the end – in one of the transepts. We can get quite close in here.' Bert moved to the side and led them down another narrow passage. It felt like they were walking parallel to the main hall and, like before, it was possible to get occasional glances through cracks in the walls. 'Why do you want to see them particularly?' he asked as they walked.

Emmie thought for a moment before replying. 'I'd heard the world's largest gem was here – star attraction or something like that,' she said.

'That's right,' replied Bert. 'There's bound to be a huge queue though.'

Jack sniffed as they continued past the back of some more stands. 'Smells like curry,' he whispered.

'We're behind the Indian section. There's tea and spices – everything our empire has to offer,' Bert explained proudly. Jack and Emmie exchanged a glance in the half-light. Neither was sure they felt as comfortable with the idea of having an empire as Bert seemed to. In fact, they had been writing a persuasive article on the topic of whether the British Empire was a good or bad thing only the week before at school. On reflection, there seemed to have been at least as many bad points as good.

'Are there things on display from all around the world?' asked Emmie.

'Yeah – all over the place,' said Bert. He peeked through the curtain backing onto the Indian stand, then turned back to them. 'A lot of the foreign things are at this end – there's some French stands over there with musical instruments and paintings, then on the other side there's some Austrian toys and Russian vases. Most of the empire stands are in the middle.'

It was that word again – empire. Emmie shuffled awkwardly and avoided Bert's gaze. 'Are you alright?' he asked, 'you were enjoying it a minute ago.'

'Just hungry,' Emmie replied, giving the boy a little smile. She didn't feel that she could explain to him why she was uncomfortable – it just seemed wrong for one country to control such a large swathe of the globe.

'Well, why didn't you say before? I can sort us out some food – just stay here a minute.' Without waiting for a reply, he melted into the background, leaving Emmie and Jack alone in the semi-darkness.

'What do you think?' asked Jack.

'About what?'

'This place. It's amazing!' Jack was peeking through the curtain that Bert had moved a few moments before. 'I want to have a proper look around.'

Emmie rolled her eyes at him in mock disapproval – Jack was always excited for the next adventure, sometimes missing the fact that they hadn't finished the one they were on yet. 'We need to focus on finding the diamond – I'm sure we'll get a chance to see some of the exhibits as we search though.'

After Hours

A rustling sound preceded Bert's return, as he reappeared carrying a large paper bag. In a narrow shaft of light, they examined his prize. 'Mmm, cake,' exclaimed Jack excitedly. 'Where did you get it from?'

Bert explained that there was a refreshment area nearby, and that he knew one of the girls who worked there. 'She's a cousin, or something like that,' he half-explained. He handed a generous slice of cake to each of them, which they eagerly munched.

'Can we... see the jewels... next,' Jack asked, through a mouthful of cake. He wiped his face with the back of his hand. 'Nice cake though.'

'Sure,' agreed Bert. 'The best way is probably from upstairs.' He pointed in the direction he'd reappeared from, telling them that the stairs were that way too. 'We'll just have to be careful getting out of here – don't want everyone to know there's a secret passage!'

Emmie and Jack followed him through the gloom, until he stopped behind another heavy curtain. 'I'll just check,' he whispered, moving the curtain slightly. He froze, then carefully let the curtain drop. They could see him put a finger to his lips, and then move sideways to get a different view. He dropped to his knees and waved at them to follow him. Slowly, they crawled forward and managed to squeeze between some wooden legs, before seeing Bert veer to the right and stand up.

They were now in a small space just off one of the main staircases. Emmie could hear people moving past and the tap-tap sound as they ascended the stairs. 'What now?' she asked quietly.

'We just step out and act like we're meant to be here,' said Bert confidently. 'Like this.' With that, he walked forward and joined the procession of people using the staircase. Emmie glanced sideways at Jack and followed.

The staircase was made of iron, with heavy wooden treads which echoed as the footsteps passed by. It was wide, with easily enough room for four people side-by-side. Two flights later, they were at the top and emerged onto a balcony – more stands stretching out in a line behind them.

'Look – there's the Queen again,' said Emmie excitedly. The royal party were on their way back through the pavilion, having been shown around the many exhibits. They came to a sudden halt in the middle of the room below, with Prince Albert holding an animated conversation with one of the royal guards. They both seemed to be looking around for something, or someone. Two further guards stood nearby, looking a little uneasy. As they watched the scene beneath them, Princess Sarah glanced up at the balcony. Instinctively, Emmie raised her hand and waved at the girl, receiving a small smile in return. 'Poor girl – she looks so bored trailing round with the adults,' she said to Jack.

'She's got a better life here than in Africa,' Bert joined in.

'What do you mean?' Emmie was curious about the girl.

'She was brought back as a gift for the Queen from some expedition to Africa. She decided to adopt her is what I heard,' explained Bert.

Emmie's head whirled – the idea of the girl being some sort of present felt appalling to her. She was a person, not something to be traded for the benefit of others. She didn't seem unhappy though – was this just how things were in the 1850's?

Jack dragged her away from her thoughts. 'Look – there's the diamond!' She gazed down at where he was pointing, and saw a crowd gathered around what appeared to be a large birdcage with a crown on top. There was a sign above the crowd which read 'World's Largest Diamond'.

'Where? Is it actually in that cage?' Emmie asked, a little burst of relief flowing through her. Maybe this wouldn't be so complicated after all?

'Yep – to stop people nicking it,' Bert told them. 'Father says the cage has a safe underneath, and it drops down into it at night.'

Emmie looked down at the crowd again – it was impossible to actually see the diamond from up here, assuming it was there at all. She wasn't quite sure what they were supposed to do when they found it either – how were they meant to stop it disappearing from their present? 'Can we get any closer?' she asked Bert. The boy shook his head slowly.

'Not unless you want to queue for ages. There are loads of other things to see anyway – why don't we come back here later?' He peered towards the far end of the pavilion, where you could see out of the huge windows into Hyde Park. 'There's musical instruments from France down there, and at the other end are model soldiers and even some guns.'

Emmie thought for a moment – it was busy, being the opening day. Maybe later would be a better choice – she didn't really want to leave it until the next day though. Now they had located where the diamond should be, she was keen to check it was there before anything went wrong.

As if reading her mind, Bert then revealed what he hoped was his great idea. 'We could always meet up this evening, when the Exhibition's closed,' he suggested. 'I could let you in again and we could have a private tour.' The boy waited for a response – he was very proud of his special access and keen to show it off again.

Emmie looked at Jack – they might not be able to see the diamond later either, as it sounded like it would be locked away, but a secret expedition could be quite an adventure. There was also a chance that they could confirm the diamond was in the safe somehow. 'Yes – let's do it,' he agreed, grinning broadly at them both.

A few moments later, a bell rang out twice. 'What's that for?' asked Emmie.

'It means the Exhibition is closing soon,' Bert explained. 'Let's leave with everyone else and then I can meet you later when it gets dark.'

*

A little later as dusk fell, Jack and Emmie quietly crunched across the gravel outside the front of the exhibition space, grateful to be on the move again. They headed for the door which Bert had let them into that afternoon. Jack reached out his hand and tried to push the door, but it was firmly closed. 'There's only a handle on the inside,' he grumbled, 'we'll have to wait...' The minutes ticked past, and Jack grew impatient. 'Where is he?'

'I don't know,' Emmie whispered back. 'I'm sure he'll come though. He seemed really excited to show us around some more.' They'd just about given up hope, when there were more footsteps on the gravel, and Bert hurried into view.

'Sorry I'm late...' he panted. 'I couldn't find the key in Father's jacket.' He took a breath and looked at the door. 'If we're lucky, it might be unlocked.'

'I've tried it – no luck,' Jack confirmed. 'Any other ideas?'

Bert thought for a minute and then his face brightened. 'There are some roof vents – we could shin up and get in that way,' he said eagerly. 'Just need to find a drainpipe to help with the climb.'

Jack stared up at the sheer glass wall – it was very high, and the top was a long way away. 'Are you sure?' he asked, feeling butterflies in his stomach. 'I don't want to get all the way up and find we can't get inside.'

'The vents are always open,' Bert assured him. 'There needs to be air circulating so the trees don't get too hot.'

Jack looked up again – he wasn't happy about the idea but didn't want to seem scared in front of Bert. 'I guess we can try—'

'Come on Jack – it'll be fine. I'll go first if you like?' Emmie's suggestion had the desired effect – Jack had no intention of letting her get the better of him either.

'Where's the drainpipe?' he asked, looking around before spotting one a few panes of glass along from where they stood.

Bert got there first and wrapped his arms around the iron pipe. 'Copy me,' he said, reaching up and pulling himself skyward like a monkey. His feet searched out the frame of each pane of glass, giving him a thin ledge to propel himself from. Jack and Emmie looked on in awe, as Bert quickly scaled two floors of the pavilion and hauled himself over the edge onto the roof.

'He made that look easy,' muttered Jack, still not totally confident about what was to come. He reached up and copied Bert's movements, climbing more slowly but still inching towards the roofline. When his fingers finally reached the decorative top edge, he allowed himself a brief smile, before rolling over the parapet and sitting up. He peered back down, seeing Emmie already half-way up the drainpipe. He gave her a quick thumbs-up and looked across at Bert.

'Just be careful up here,' the boy warned. 'You need to stay on the metal parts – the glass isn't strong enough to stand on.' Jack peered down – he was sat on a metal girder which formed the main frame of the pavilion. Thin spars stretched upwards, forming the arch of the roof, and holding panes of glass in place. He would have to stay on the main girder as much as possible, as the spars were really slender.

Emmie heaved herself onto the roof at that point, and Jack reiterated Bert's warning. She glanced around and saw the roof vents just above them. 'Look!' she cried, 'they're open!' Something else caught her eye too – there was a small orange glow coming from below them, deep inside the pavilion. As she looked, the light flickered, and she realised it must be a candle. But who would have lit one in a deserted exhibition hall? Unless it wasn't deserted after all...

The Diamond Disappears

'What's that?' Emmie whispered, pointing towards the flickering light far below them. As she strained to see in the darkness, she thought there was a hunched figure visible in the candlelight.

'Someone's down there, aren't they?' agreed Jack. He looked around on the roof – they'd have to crawl along the main girder, then somehow navigate one of the narrow frames to get to the roof vent.

Bert seemed one step ahead of him and was already moving along the girder. 'Come this way, but be careful,' he urged quietly. The three children slowly crawled along the edge of the roof, feeling out for the cold iron girder, and trying not to look over the edge. You couldn't see much in the dark, but it still felt very high up. Bert reached the frame they'd have to balance on and stopped to look. It was really thin – only about five centimetres across. He sucked air through his teeth as he considered it – one slip and he'd crack the glass...

'It's like a tightrope – you just need to keep your balance,' said Emmie, sounding way more confident than she felt. The others stared at her blankly, so she stood and put her arms out wide, like an acrobat in the circus. Tentatively putting one foot ahead of the other, she took a step onto the frame, hardly daring to breathe. She waited for the crack of the glass, and to feel the sensation of falling, but it held. She took a breath and carefully swung her other leg around, placing that foot in front of the first one. Still no crack.

'Go on, Emmie,' Jack urged quietly behind her. She smiled to herself and moved forward again. Ten further steps and she was at the roof vent. It sat just under the ridgeline of the roof which, thankfully, was made of a thicker piece of iron. As long as she could get to it, sitting down and sliding through the vent should be simple. One more step. She tried to block everything from her mind and gently moved forward, before pivoting and sitting on the ridge. Grinning with relief, she beckoned to Jack and Bert.

As Bert started to make his way along the white-painted frame, Emmie looked down through the vent. Luckily, there was a display stand right underneath it. If she could drop through at the right angle, it was only a couple of metres to the stand roof. She tried to calculate it in her head – was it too far? After a moment pondering, she took the plunge and sat down onto the edge of the vent. Feeling a momentary wobble as her feet dangled in mid-air, she gritted her teeth and pushed herself through, landing squarely on the roof of the stand. 'Ouch!' she grimaced quietly to herself, feeling her ankle jar with the impact. She rubbed it through her long skirt, glad that it wasn't really hurt.

Conscious that her landing must have made some noise, Emmie froze and listened. There seemed to be no other movement around her, so she slowly crept to the edge of the stand roof and peered down. The moon was out, casting a gentle light over the pavilion, and she was able to see the figure far below, dressed in a red jacket and holding a candle. She watched intently as the figure focused on their task, too far away to see exactly what was going on. A gentle thud from behind caused her to turn around, and she saw Jack crouching on the stand roof too. She beckoned him over to her and pointed down to the figure.

'What do you think they're doing?' Jack whispered. 'It's a bit odd being here in the dark, with just a candle.'

'Unless they don't want to be seen?' suggested Emmie. 'Maybe they're—'

CRASH! A sudden noise made the pair jump, and the roof they were crouching on shook. As Emmie whirled round to see that Bert had made a heavier than planned entrance, she caught sight of a flash of red moving beneath them. 'How did you manage that?!' she hissed at the boy, then turned back to check on the figure, who had now predictably vanished.

'Shh!' said Jack urgently, straining to hear the receding footsteps. There was the unmistakeable sound of a door slamming, which echoed around the glass walls long after it had happened.

'I'm sorry...' Bert was very uncomfortable at having caused this particular issue. 'I slipped on the frame and couldn't stop myself.'

'Well, at least you're not hurt,' said Emmie graciously. There was a pause. 'Are you hurt?' she asked, feeling a bit mean that she'd just assumed he was all right.

Bert looked up at her. 'I'm fine. What do you want to do now though?'

'I'd like to know what that person was doing. I've got a feeling they were up to something they shouldn't have been.' Emmie sensed this was maybe going to complicate things for them quite a bit. She swung her legs over the side of the stand and dropped to the floor, looking back up at the two boys, who quickly followed her. Once on the ground, she moved over to the balcony edge and peered down.

'I knew it!' she said triumphantly. 'That person was doing something with the diamond – look, they were right by the cage.'

Bert pointed down the gallery. 'There are some stairs - let's get a closer look.' They hurried down the staircase, less worried about making noise now, and raced to the cage in the centre of the wide aisle.

'It's not there,' said Emmie. 'Where did it go?'

'Remember the safe?' Bert said. 'The diamond is designed to drop down into it at night.'

'Well, it's not there now...' announced Jack, who had got down on his knees to inspect the safe. 'It's empty.'

'What do you mean – empty?' said Emmie in disbelief.

Jack just pointed at the safe door, which hung open. There was a tiny space inside – just large enough for the diamond. And totally bare.

Emmie and Jack looked at each other in stunned silence. It was obvious now – the figure with the candle must have stolen the diamond. It had happened right in front of them. Emmie put her hands up to her face, a cold chill creeping through her body. They had no obvious way of getting home and had assumed finding the diamond would somehow unlock a route back. If it had been stolen instead of just lost, then their chances of getting it back were now infinitely smaller. Her mind raced – would they now have to try and figure out who the thief was? Where would they even start?

'If only we'd got in a bit earlier...' Jack said slowly, echoing her thoughts. Emmie could hear the disappointment in his voice and felt momentarily annoyed that Bert had taken so long looking for the key. She knew it wasn't fair to blame the boy when he had been so helpful, but the consequences of the delay could be huge.

'We should get out of here,' Bert muttered. 'I don't want to get caught inside after something like this. We could get framed for it.' His last comment stirred Jack and Emmie into action – neither wanted to spend any more time in the police cells.

'How do we get out then?' asked Jack. 'Do we have to go back through the air vent?' He shuddered a bit at the thought – it had been very high, and he didn't really want to repeat the experience.

Bert started walking back towards the main entrance. 'We can use the door from earlier,' he said over his shoulder. 'They open from the inside, remember – come on.' Nearing the front of the pavilion, Bert abruptly stopped, then waved Jack and Emmie towards the wall of a stand displaying cotton fabric. 'Stay still,' he hissed.

Jack looked around them – the pavilion was quiet, and he couldn't work out what had spooked Bert. 'What is it?' he asked softly.

Bert pointed through the glazing and out into the park. 'Lights - someone's coming to investigate. We need to go right now.' He slipped down the side of the cotton stand and away from the front doors, checking over his shoulder to make sure Jack and Emmie were following. A few further steps took them to the side door Bert had let them in through earlier.

Pausing briefly with his hand on the handle, Bert looked around. He strained his eyes to see if there was any movement outside, then apparently satisfied, he gently opened the door. It moved soundlessly on its hinges, swinging open into the moonlight. 'Quick!' he hissed, fearful that there could be more people on the way. Jack and Emmie followed him out of the door and crouched down as he quietly closed it. Listening hard, they could now hear the crunch of footsteps on the gravel at the front of the pavilion.

'Probably time to split up,' suggested Jack. 'It might be safer if we're not all together.'

Bert nodded. 'I'm going home – I don't want Father to know I've been out. Not now this has happened.'

'Will we see you again?' asked Emmie, hoping that they would.

'I'll be here tomorrow, like normal,' Bert said, sounding more cheerful than he felt at that moment. 'Don't get caught.' With that he was off, bent low and running across the park – back to wherever he lived.

'Come on,' said Jack, 'let's go over to the Serpentine – we can watch from there and see what happens next.'

The Missing Guard

As they sat by the large lake in the centre of the park, with the gentle sound of water lapping behind them, Emmie glanced over at Jack. In the moonlight, his face under the cap looked even more comical than it had done the day before. The day before – had it really only been yesterday that they had been flung into this adventure?

'Look – you can see them now,' he whispered, looking through the trees and back towards the great glass building.

Emmie narrowed her eyes and looked where he indicated. There were a number of men in red tunics approaching the pavilion. They were obviously soldiers, by the way they were marching in line. Something rang a little bell in the back of her mind – was the man they'd seen earlier a soldier too? He'd been dressed the same as these men, for sure. 'Could the thief have been a soldier, do you think?' Emmie asked quietly. 'It might have been easier for them to get access to the pavilion.'

Now Jack was thinking too. 'Remember that fuss when the Queen was about to leave earlier? I'm sure there were only three guards then, but four arrived with them.' He took off the cap for a moment and ran his hand through his orange hair. 'Well, even if it was a soldier, we'd have no chance of working out which one. I must have seen at least fifty today alone.'

'I think we should come back in the morning and see what's going on then,' suggested Emmie. 'There are people crawling all over the Exhibition tonight and hopefully they might turn up some clues. We could even find the diamond is back safe and sound tomorrow.'

'Will that be enough though?' Jack asked. 'We still don't really know what we have to do to get it back in the present.'

Emmie shook her head slowly. 'I don't know,' she admitted. 'I really wish we'd asked Mr Briggs more questions earlier. He didn't really give us any chance in the police station though.'

Jack scratched his head – it was late, and the chance of them finding a room for the night was slim, even if they had some money. It didn't feel too cold, despite being clear. He looked across at Emmie, who yawned in response. 'Should we just sleep out here tonight? There's a bench over there, and it's pretty quiet.' She nodded at the suggestion, slightly surprised at herself for agreeing to sleep on a park bench but, in reality, nothing about their adventures was ever very normal.

*

The gentle dawn light roused Jack, dancing over his eyelids and causing him to roll over in an effort to escape it. He suddenly found himself fully awake and face down on the gravel path, having rolled right off the bench. 'Uhhh,' he sighed, lifting his face up and brushing bits of stone off it. He glanced over at Emmie, who still appeared to be sleeping peacefully, and dragged himself back onto the bench. His stomach growled in the still morning air – first priority had to be finding some breakfast. He looked over at the pavilion and saw that the glass had a pinkish hue reflecting from the sunrise. There were quite a few people about, considering it was so early, and many of them appeared to be heading into the Exhibition. It couldn't be open already, so they must be workers – what Jack knew by now was that, where workers congregated, there was generally food. He leaned over and shook Emmie by the shoulder.

'Huh? What's going on...?' she murmured sleepily, opening one eye and then closing it again.

'Fancy some breakfast?' Jack asked. That got a reaction, as Emmie sat up, rubbing the sleep from her eyes.

She looked at him – a mixture of excitement and doubt in her expression, wondering if he actually had a plan to get some food, or was just using it to rouse her. 'What's for breakfast then?' she asked, humouring him.

He pointed at the steady stream of workers entering the pavilion. 'There's bound to be something to eat in there – let's go and find it.' They walked across the grass together, feet squelching as it was still damp from the morning dew. There was a sooty smell in the air – no doubt the result of thousands of coal fires burning in nearby houses – but the park still seemed fresh at the start of a new day.

As they reached the door, Jack turned to her and whispered quietly. 'Just act like we belong here.'

'I have done that once or twice before,' Emmie laughed in reply.

Filing in through the great doors, alongside quiet groups of workers, Jack gazed around. There were people sweeping up, carrying boxes, and cleaning the large panes of glass. He sniffed - there was definitely food cooking somewhere nearby. Walking through the pavilion with purpose, his nose led him to a sausage stand which had opened early. Joining the queue of hungry people, Jack noticed that no money seemed to be changing hands – this was obviously some sort of free breakfast put on for the early morning workers. He shuffled forward and put his hand out for a plate of sausages and bread when it was offered. The man behind the stand looked slightly suspicious but handed over the food all the same.

Passing the plate to Emmie, Jack guided them round a corner and away from the gaze of the sausage vendor. They hungrily tucked into the food, glad of something warm inside to start the day.

'We should go and see the diamond exhibit,' said Emmie when they had finished. 'We need to know what happened last night, or at least what the situation is now.'

As they approached the great cage in the middle of the pavilion, Emmie could see something sparkling inside, the sunlight dancing around it in waves.

'Look!' exclaimed Jack excitedly.

'Don't get too carried away, son. It's not the real one,' muttered a man sweeping the floor nearby.

Jack looked at him in confusion. 'What do you mean?' he asked, nearly adding that he knew the gem had vanished, but thinking better of it.

'Got nicked last night, didn't it?' said the man, looking furtively around. 'Only they don't want to admit that the star attraction is missing and lose all those ticket sales. At least Her Majesty is coming back again today – that'll bring the crowds in.'

He moved away, and Emmie nodded knowingly at Jack. 'Well, it's definitely gone then, hasn't it?'

Jack stared into the distance for a moment, before answering. 'I wonder...' he said, 'if the mysteriously disappearing guard will be back today or not?'

'I don't understand,' answered Emmie.

'Well,' said Jack, picking up his idea from the night before. 'Remember how animated Prince Albert was yesterday when the royal party were about to leave?' Emmie nodded, so he continued. 'I'm convinced they were missing one of the guards. I wonder if he had anything to do with it... It's a bit odd to just vanish when you're on royal duty.'

Emmie caught up now – Jack might be onto something here. 'The person last night was definitely wearing a red tunic,' she said. 'The royal guards dress like that too, so it could have been the same person. There are a lot of soldiers about though...'

'Either way, I think we should wait around and see. If one of the guards was involved, I bet they'll look pretty nervous today.' Jack was keen to prove his theory one way or the other.

*

By 11 o'clock, the exhibition space was thronging with people, all excitedly looking at the displays of goods and inventions. There was hardly room to move, and the queue around the diamond cage was just as big as the previous day. From the far end of the pavilion came the sound of a trumpeter, and a hush descended amongst the crowd. They knew this meant the arrival of the Queen, and everyone was eager to catch a glimpse of her. There was no chance of Jack and Emmie getting any closer inside the packed room.

'Through here,' Jack said, grabbing Emmie's arm and leading her behind a nearby stand displaying carriage clocks. He parted a curtain, and she recognised the space between the stands which Bert had showed them yesterday.

'Well done,' she said quietly, pleased that this might let them see the royal party after all. Jack led the way behind a row of stands, peeking through any gaps to check their progress. Just after they had passed the Indian spice stand, he stopped and gently moved the curtain aside. No more than three metres away, Queen Victoria stood, listening intently to a man explaining an invention for railway locomotives. On impulse, he stepped forward, squeezing between the stands and coming out at the edge of the crowd. Looking back at Emmie, he beckoned her to follow. As she emerged, Princess Sarah, who had been standing behind the Queen, turned and saw her. Emmie froze, worried that she had been seen slipping out from the secret passage, but the girl just smiled shyly at her. Emmie grinned back, wondering again if she was bored of behaving so formally.

'Look,' hissed Jack, pulling her focus away from Sarah, 'they've got four guards again.'

The Royal Toilet

Emmie stared at Jack – he was right, there were four royal guards once again. What did that mean? Had one been missing after all? Was it even related to the man they'd observed the night before? So many questions, and it wasn't clear where they were going to find any answers either.

The royal party moved onwards, guided once more by a uniformed attendant who listened intently to what the Queen showed an interest in seeing. As they walked past, Sarah turned in Emmie's direction again, giving her another little smile.

'I'd like to ask her what went on when they were trying to leave yesterday,' said Emmie. 'I bet she'd be able to give us a clue or two.'

'Clue about what?' came a voice at their side, and Emmie turned to see Bert standing there.

'Oh Bert! Did you get home all right?' she asked him. 'I hope you didn't get into trouble being out so late?'

Bert grinned at her, exposing a row of slightly crooked teeth. 'Nah – they were all asleep when I got home. I was there in the morning – that's all that matters. Anyway, what about this clue?'

Emmie hesitated briefly, then decided sticking as close to the truth as possible was the best thing to do. 'We think that trouble yesterday when the royal party was leaving might have been because one of the guards was missing. We were wondering whether it was anything to do with the man we saw last night.' She paused, seeing Bert nod thoughtfully. 'I said I'd like to ask the princess if she knew what was going on. Obviously, that's impossible...' her voice trailed off.

'Well, you say that, but nothing's really impossible,' boasted Bert. 'You just need to know who to ask.'

Emmie looked at him, wondering what he meant. 'Who do we need to ask?'

'Me, of course! I know all the little secrets of this place. I'll get you close enough to her to ask your question.'

It seemed too good to be true. Surely someone would stop them from just walking up to Sarah and starting a conversation? Bert's enthusiasm was infectious though, and Emmie found herself getting caught up in it. 'Ok then,' she agreed, 'show us what you can do.'

'Give me five minutes,' came the reply, as Bert slipped back between the stands and disappeared.

*

'Follow me please,' called a voice nearby. There was a pause and then it came again. 'Sir and Madam – yes, you please.' Emmie felt a gentle dig in her ribs and looked around. A young boy dressed as a waiter stood next to them, looking expectantly in their direction.

Emmie chuckled. 'Bert! What are you wearing that for?'

'All part of the plan,' he replied, looking very pleased with himself. 'Now, if you'd like to follow me please.' He led them through the crowded space and into the refreshment court. It was ornately decorated, with carved screens and tropical plants in pots. White painted tables and chairs were laid out in little groups, with people sat eating and waiters attending to them. He led the pair to a table in one corner, next to a large, circular table which was arranged on a raised platform.

'Thanks,' said Emmie. 'How does this help us talk to Sarah though?'

'Ah,' the boy replied, 'that table next to you is for the Queen. She'll be in here shortly for refreshments.'

'Clever,' Emmie acknowledged. 'How about—'

What she was about to say never got finished, as Bert was hailed by a man in a long frock coat at a nearby table. 'Here, waiter.'

'Be back soon,' said Bert quietly, as he hurried away.

Emmie gazed around the room before turning to Jack. 'Wow – this is amazing, isn't it? To think we'll be having tea next to the Queen!'

Jack nodded. 'What do you think Sarah will be able to tell us?' he mused. 'I can't imagine she'll know who stole the diamond.'

'No, me either,' Emmie replied, 'but she may be able to tell us what happened with that missing guard, and that might give us a clue.'

'We still need to know how this ends,' Jack reminded her. 'I mean – do we just have to find out where the diamond is, or do something particular with it? There's 170 years of history between now and the present – a lot could happen in that time.'

Emmie sighed. 'I wish I knew. I think the main priority must be to find out what has happened to it though.'

At that moment, a hush descended on the refreshment room as the diners noticed the royal party approaching. Emmie saw that everyone sat up straight and looked respectfully in the direction of the Queen as she passed through the room. Once seated, Emmie was pleased to see that Sarah was on the side of the large table nearest to them.

'How are you going to approach her?' Jack whispered. 'You can't exactly just walk up to the table, can you?'

Emmie wasn't sure – she hadn't really thought this far ahead and had just been going along with Bert's suggestion so far. Thankfully, the boy reappeared and began to put his grand plan into action. Carrying a tall tray of sandwiches behind some other waiters, he approached the royal table and placed them down. Working around the guests, he unfolded napkins and offered to lay them across their laps. As he did this to Sarah, he appeared to whisper something briefly into her ear, before quickly moving on.

A few minutes later, the girl excused herself from the table and headed for a curtained-off area at the back of the room. Emmie caught Bert's eye as he came back from the kitchen, and he inclined his head in the direction Sarah had gone in. 'Be back in a minute,' she said quietly to Jack as she got up, peered furtively around, and headed for the back of the room.

As she reached the curtain, Emmie could see that a middle-aged lady-in-waiting was standing to one side of it, apparently to stop people wandering in. The lady was talking to one of the waiters and, having quickly looked behind her to make sure no-one on the royal table could see, Emmie teased open the other end of the curtain and slipped behind it.

Staring around the space behind the curtain, Emmie's eyes boggled. If the rest of the exhibition hall was grand, then this was ridiculously opulent. The walls were covered in silk drapes, with carefully positioned screens near the windows to allow light in, but also maintain privacy. A cluster of deep red velvet armchairs sat in one corner, with a carved wooden sideboard nearby. In the other corner, a small room had been constructed, complete with panelled door and gold handle. Emmie heard a flushing sound and realised the room must be a bathroom. The handle turned, and her stomach lurched a bit – hopefully it would be Sarah who emerged...

The door opened and the two girls came face-to-face. Emmie felt relieved, but Sarah looked very shocked at finding someone else in this private zone. She opened her mouth to speak, but Emmie got there first.

'I'm sorry for bursting in,' she started, 'but I just needed to speak to you for a minute.'

Sarah's eyes were wide, and she kept glancing towards the curtain, where Emmie knew the lady-in-waiting was stood just the other side. Emmie kept her voice low, so as not to be overheard. 'May I ask you a question please?'

Tense moments passed as the girls stared at each other, both trying to decide what to do next. Finally, Sarah spoke, smoothing down her skirt as she did so. 'Yes, you may. But then you have to leave.'

Emmie smiled gratefully at the girl. 'Thank you. I wanted to know about the guard who disappeared last night. What happened to him?'

Sarah's eyes narrowed at this question, and Emmie could tell she was surprised to be asked it. There was a pause before the girl answered. 'He disappeared while we were visiting the Exhibition yesterday and no-one could find him when we were ready to leave.'

'Did he come back again?' asked Emmie. 'I noticed that there were four guards again this morning.'

'Yes, he did,' confirmed Sarah. 'He was here this morning, though there's something a little odd about him.'

'How do you mean?' Emmie pressed.

Sarah glanced nervously at the curtain again. 'I really have to go,' she said.

'Please.' Emmie looked desperately at her – she had to find out what the girl knew.

'His voice is just different to normal somehow.' Sarah sighed, her shoulders drooping a little, before walking out through the curtain, leaving Emmie to puzzle over her answer.

She didn't have long to think though, as the curtain twitched in front of her. Someone was coming in! She quickly stepped into the bathroom and closed the door behind her, quietly locking the door. The space was small and contained a white porcelain toilet bowl, set in an elaborate wooden surround. It looked more like a throne than a toilet, with a blue floral decoration on the visible parts of the porcelain. Emmie had never seen anything quite like it before.

The door handle suddenly rattled, making her jump. Heart beating wildly, she tried to hold her breath, conscious of making even the smallest noise. The handle rattled again, then stopped, and she heard footsteps receding. Bending down and putting her eye to the keyhole, she could just about make out the shape of the lady-in-waiting passing back through the curtain. Realising that the woman had likely gone to get some help for what she imagined was a stuck door, Emmie quickly let herself out and headed back to the opposite end of the curtain. She gently peered around it, seeing that the refreshment room was slightly emptier now.

Taking a deep breath, and stepping out from behind the curtain with a confidence that she didn't feel, Emmie walked shakily back across the room to Jack. 'Let's get out of here,' she said to him, barely stopping at the table.

14

To The Palace!

'What's the matter?' asked Jack, as they crossed the refreshment room and headed back into the exhibition. 'You look like you've seen a ghost.'

She turned to face him, exhaling slowly before she spoke. 'Not exactly. But I did nearly get caught in the Queen's loo...'

'You what?!' Jack spluttered; laughter written all over his face. 'No way!'

'I managed to get into the room behind that curtain, but it was empty,' Emmie explained, recounting how grand the furnishings had been. 'Then Sarah came out of a little room, and I realised it was the royal toilet.'

Jack was still grinning at the thought of this. 'So how did you nearly get caught then?'

'Well,' Emmie replied, 'when Sarah had gone, someone else came, so I hid in the toilet. The first thing they did was try the door. Luckily, they went away, and I was able to slip out.'

After a moment, Jack's grin faded as he remembered the real reason for Emmie's little adventure. 'Did you speak to her then? Did she tell you anything?'

'Thought you'd never ask,' Emmie retorted, the panicked feeling having subsided now. 'I managed to speak to Sarah, though I thought she was going to shriek when she first saw me. She obviously wasn't expecting to find someone waiting for her when she came out of the toilet.'

'And?' said Jack, impatiently.

'Something and nothing, I think. She just said the guard had disappeared but was back this morning. She did say that his voice was a bit strange though – I didn't really understand what she meant by that.'

Jack looked thoughtful for a moment. 'Doesn't really help us know whether the guard was involved or not though, does it?'

Emmie shook her head slowly. 'Not really... I wonder though – if he did steal the diamond, what would he have done next? It was the middle of the night—' She stopped suddenly, and a strange look passed over her face. 'What if he still has it? Hidden somewhere safe maybe, but close by so he can retrieve it later?'

'Maybe...' Jack said doubtfully. 'But where? How do you even begin to second guess something like that?'

Emmie's eyes sparkled now – she thought she was onto something, and enthusiasm was taking over. 'The palace,' she said, 'it's got to be – that's where the guards live, and no-one's going to be poking around in there, are they?'

'Ok,' said Jack, 'suppose you're right. How do we get into Buckingham Palace to find it? Not exactly somewhere you can just walk into, is it?'

It was as if he had just deflated a tyre. Emmie's face fell, her shoulders slumped, and the corners of her mouth turned down. 'We could ask Bert to help again...' she said quietly.

'Bert? I really don't think he's got connections in the royal household!' Jack said, sounding a bit harsher than he'd meant to.

'Ah – there you both are. I thought I heard my name.' Bert approached them from the direction of the refreshment room. 'Did you manage to get what you needed?'

'Yes, I think so,' confirmed Emmie, grateful for the boy's help so far. Something behind him caused her to look up, and her face froze for a second.

'Are you alright?' Bert asked, turning to see what she was looking at. A few metres away, a tall man stood, dressed in a black morning suit, and wearing a top hat. This didn't really set him apart from many of the other male visitors, but Emmie knew exactly who he was.

'Hello Mr Briggs,' she said, presuming the name the man had given them earlier was still the right one to use. Her pulse quickened as he walked across to them – he had said before that he was able to help when they were in difficulties – were they in some sort of trouble now?

'Good morning. Would I be able to have a word with the two of you please?' said Mr Briggs. He looked pointedly at Bert, who shifted uncomfortably on his feet.

'Uh, well I'd better be getting on then...' he said, looking a bit disappointed at being asked to leave.

'Thanks Bert. We'll see you later.' Emmie felt bad for him too, but they really needed to have this conversation. It might make all the difference.

'Walk with me,' suggested Mr Briggs, 'it's best we're not overheard.' He led them away into the main gallery, politely working through the crowds until they reached a quieter area near one of the huge glass walls. Jack peered out of the window and realised it overlooked the benches they'd spent the previous night sleeping on. 'How are you?' asked Mr Briggs. 'How much progress have you made?'

Emmie breathed a little easier – they obviously weren't in trouble after all. 'Well,' she replied, 'we know the diamond has been stolen – we saw it happen.'

'You saw it?' the man replied excitedly. 'Well, that's a good start. Who took it? Could you identify them?'

Emmie shrugged her shoulders. 'We don't know. We were on the roof, looking down. All we could really see was a figure with a candle, wearing a red tunic.'

'But he might have been a royal guard,' Jack added.

Mr Briggs looked quizzical. 'A guard? How do you know that?'

'One of the royal guards disappeared yesterday when the Queen came to open the Exhibition. Sarah told us he'd come back but was behaving a bit strangely.' Jack flushed, pleased with himself at being able to provide this important piece of information.

'Who is Sarah, if you don't mind me asking?'

Emmie took over the explanation now. 'Princess Sarah – she's apparently an adopted daughter of the Queen.'

'Well I never!' Mr Briggs was almost lost for words. 'You two are getting very good at this. Did you ever imagine having a conversation with one of Queen Victoria's family? How did you manage that?'

'Bert helped a lot,' said Emmie. 'He's that boy we were just talking to – he knows the inside of this place really well.' She took a deep breath and then continued. 'What we really need though is to get inside Buckingham Palace and search that guard's room.'

Mr Briggs stared at her with an expression she took to be disbelief. He shook his head slowly, then a smile broke out on his face. 'Ok, then. What are we waiting for?'

'We do need you to tell us what to do when we find the diamond,' said Emmie. 'We know that it needs finding, but what then? Does it just have to be put back, or something more?'

'The truth is, I didn't know what was needed until you just confirmed it had been stolen,' Mr Briggs replied. 'It had disappeared in the present, but I couldn't tell why. Now we know it has been stolen everything makes sense. Once it is back at the Exhibition then all will be well.'

'And the coronation can take place?' Emmie added.

'Yes,' Mr Briggs smiled again. 'Now let me help you with the palace.'

*

Walking out of Hyde Park and along the busy pavement, Jack felt curiously free. Maybe it was the relief at being outside again, or possibly the thought that they were closer to solving the mystery of the diamond than they had been before. The sky was clear – or it would have been if there wasn't so much coal smoke in the air. A perpetual grey tinge seemed to hang over everything, no matter how bright the sun might be. Jack cleared his throat – as nice as it was to be outside, he would rather breathe the cleaner London air he was used to than from this polluted sky.

As they rounded the corner onto Grosvenor Place and started to walk behind the grounds of Buckingham Palace, Jack began to wonder how they were actually going to get inside. Quite rightly, he imagined the palace to be secure, and not somewhere one could just walk into. As it turned out, the solution Mr Briggs had seemed rather simple after all.

'Are you ready?' he asked, as they passed a nondescript wooden gate in the high wall.

'I think so,' Jack replied. 'Ready for what though?' he added after a moment.

Mr Briggs looked around, then reached into his pocket and brought out a bunch of keys. As he sorted through them a large cart trundled into view, pulled by two black shire horses. It stopped across the road from them, the horses whinnying to each other. The cart was carrying barrels, and a man with a battered bowler hat sat on the front, loosely holding the reins. Mr Briggs looked up and furrowed his brow. 'I'm supposed to be somewhere else now,' he said – more to himself than anyone else. He handed the bunch of keys to Jack, holding them by a long, slightly rusty key. 'You'll have to do this part yourselves,' he said, before swiftly walking away and disappearing amongst the other pedestrians on the pavement.

'What was that all about?' Jack asked, slightly bemused by the man's departure. 'I guess he left us the keys at least.' He glanced up and down the pavement, before reaching behind him and working the long key into the lock of the green painted gate. There was a rattling noise, but the gate didn't open. Jack grunted and tried again, trying to look inconspicuous as he did so.

'It's not the right key, is it?' asked Emmie. 'Maybe that was just the one he happened to be holding?' Jack rolled his eyes at her and tried a second key, fumbling a bit as he searched behind him for the keyhole. The second key didn't even seem to fit into the hole. Tutting to himself, Jack went through the rest of the bunch with similarly disappointing results.

'What now...?' he grumbled. 'None of them work.'

'Excuse me,' said a voice to his left. Jack turned to see a lamplighter trying to lean his ladder against the streetlight next to the gate.

'Sorry,' he muttered, stepping aside.

CRASH! Jack and Emmie jerked around to see the source of the sudden noise. A barrel had fallen off the cart opposite them and was careering across the road. There was a shout of alarm and then a crunching of wood as the barrel smashed into the wheel of a carriage coming the other way. Almost in slow motion, everyone on the pavement seemed to gather around the accident, trying to get a closer look. A second barrel rolled off the cart and scattered the crowd, before coming to rest in the middle of the road. There was even more shouting, and a couple of men ran over to the cart to help secure the rest of the barrels.

Jack looked at Emmie with excitement in his eyes. 'This is our chance,' he said, pointing at the wall.

'What do you mean?' Emmie asked.

'The ladder!' Jack said impatiently. It was leaning against the lamp post where the lamplighter had left it. He was in the centre of the road still, having a good look at the traffic chaos. 'I think we can reach the top of the wall. No-one's looking – come on!'

The Palace Gardens

Taking one last look around, Jack stepped onto the ladder and began to climb. It wobbled slightly as he reached the top and leaned across to the wall. The top of the wall was slightly higher than the lamp post, but he managed to stretch and reach it. He sat astride the top for a moment – just long enough to see Emmie begin to climb behind him, then dropped down the other side.

'Oof,' he grunted as he hit the ground, joined swiftly by Emmie. 'Did anyone see you?' he asked, brushing the dirt from his knees where he had landed.

'No – they were all too busy staring at the accident still,' she confirmed. 'Quite high though, wasn't it?'

They looked around, and Jack was disappointed to find himself facing a large hedge.

'I thought we were in the palace grounds?' he grumbled. 'This isn't very impressive.'

Emmie smiled. 'Let's follow the hedge round and then see.' She pointed off to the right, where the hedge slowly curved away from them. After about fifty metres, the hedge stopped abruptly, and the pair found themselves gazing over a lake with an island in the middle. Through the trees which surrounded the lake, it was possible to see a giant building in yellow stone, with grand columns and a magnificent central dome.

'Wow! Look at that – it's really impressive from this side,' exclaimed Jack excitedly. 'I wonder how we get inside?' He peered through the trees again, scanning the rear of the palace. 'Shall we get a bit closer so we can see better?' There was a wooded area running to their right, which extended most of the way to the palace, and it was this that Jack suggested they use for cover. A series of gravel paths ran through the trees, and they set off along one, walking carefully to avoid their footsteps making too much noise.

'I think we should stay off the path,' said Emmie, after a few moments. 'There's bound to be people out here – gardeners and other staff. We're making too much noise and I don't want to risk getting into any more trouble with the police.' Jack pulled a bit of a face but stepped onto the grass alongside the path anyway. As it turned out, this was at just the right time, as Emmie spotted something ahead and stopped in her tracks. 'Get down!' she hissed. Peering through the trees, they could see an older man with a wheelbarrow further along the path – he was facing the other way, but they couldn't pass him.

Jack looked hurriedly around – to their left was a slight downward slope and a row of large bushes with purple flowers. 'I wonder if we could move along behind them?' he said quietly. 'We'd have to crouch, but I think the slope might stop us being seen.' He moved in a half-waddle, half-crouch motion behind the bushes, causing Emmie to choke back a giggle at how silly he looked. He beckoned her to join him, waving urgently as he had seen the gardener start to pick up his wheelbarrow.

Emmie tried to perform a more graceful move over to Jack, but this failed miserably when she slipped and slid down the slope on her side. 'Oh no!' she muttered, looking down at the smear of mud running all the way down her skirt. She glanced upwards at where Jack was crouching, still watching the gardener intently. He indicated that they should start moving along behind the bushes, concentrating so hard on the gardener's movements that he had entirely missed the opportunity to laugh at her fall. They slowly shuffled alongside the greenery, risking the occasional look upwards to check the man's position.

After ten or so metres, there was a gap in the bushes and their cover ran out. Jack held his hand up for Emmie to stop, then slowly raised his head to peer around the end bush. The gardener was staring right at them! Jack froze, his heart hammering in his chest so loudly that he was sure the gardener would be able to hear it. The man continued to look directly at him, unblinking, whilst Jack held his breath and waited for the inevitable shout. The gardener's eyes narrowed, then he reached down, bringing a pair of shears up to eye-level. As Jack knelt there, the man opened the shears and took a considered snip out of the bush in front of his face. Jack flinched, then realised what was going on – the gardener wasn't looking at him at all. In fact, he was only interested in the leaves directly ahead of him. This meant he wasn't focused on Jack, who was effectively invisible again.

'What's going on?' whispered Emmie, at his side. Jack lowered his head, before turning to answer her.

'He's cutting the bush right opposite us. I can see him, but he's not looking at us.'

'Should we move now?'

'We're going to have to. Once he looks through the leaves, instead of at them, he'll see us.' Jack gauged the distance to the next bush – it was about five paces away. 'I think we're going to have to crawl,' he said.

They dropped down onto their stomachs, before hearing a confused shout from the other side of the bush. 'Who's that?' the voice said, slightly unsteadily. Jack groaned inwardly – he might have known this was too good to be true. As they lay on the damp grass, faces almost touching the turf, he hoped the gardener had been calling to someone else. 'What are you doing?' the voice came again, stronger this time and with an irritated edge to it. Jack risked lifting his head a fraction and was rewarded by seeing a worn pair of black boots through the base of the hedge. The feet they belonged to were taking a step in their direction – it was time to go.

'On three,' Jack hissed to Emmie, putting his hands flat on the ground alongside him ready to push up. 'One... Two...' He saw the feet getting closer. 'Three!' He jumped up into a half-crouch and began to run away across the grass. After a few paces, he turned and saw Emmie was following. The gardener had appeared from behind the bushes and stood staring at them, not quite sure whether to give chase or not.

'That's it. You run!' His voice carried through the air behind them, causing Jack to find some extra speed. He dodged around a large ash tree, risking another look to make sure Emmie was following.

'Head for the wall,' he panted, seeing Emmie nod breathlessly. They ran straight, then veered behind a bed of tall flowers before Jack slowed a little.

Emmie caught him up. 'Why are we going towards the wall?' she asked. 'We need to find a way into the palace still.'

Jack grinned at her. 'It'll be easier if that gardener thinks we've left though. We don't want loads of people out here searching for some intruders.'

Emmie nodded slowly, impressed with his logic. 'Best lay low somewhere for a bit then, I suppose?' She looked around – the gardens were more overgrown on this side, and the bushes gave a bit of cover. 'Let's try in here?'

They pushed their way into the undergrowth, trying not to leave a trail. As the bushes closed around them, the light faded a little and their eyes had to adjust to the gloom. 'There's some sort of building over there,' Jack said quietly. 'I wonder if we should hide up until it gets dark properly?'

'It'll give us some time to clean up and think of a plan,' she agreed.

Creeping further forward, they discovered it was a playhouse which was falling apart with age. The wooden plank walls were green and cracked, and the little window had long since lost all the panes of glass. When they got there, Emmie felt an ache across her shoulders and realised she had been tensed the whole time. She reached out a hand for the small wooden door and tried the handle. Creakingly, it opened inwards, revealing a dusty space. As they entered, stooping a little to get through the door, she saw that the interior had a table and chairs, with a little cot and some wooden toys. Jack pushed the door shut behind them and they sat down, eyes adjusting to the semi-darkness.

'Well, we're unlikely to be seen in here anyway,' Jack said, as he reached for a cloth which lay on the cot. He began to wipe his trousers, then handed the cloth to Emmie to clean up her skirt. Looking slightly less grubby, the pair settled down to wait for dusk.

*

Emmie shook Jack, who had dozed off in the shadows. The window in front of them showed the darkening sky through the trees. Light outside was fading fast, and this was probably the right time for them to move around unseen. 'So, how are we going to do this?' she asked.

'Dunno, really,' admitted Jack, who had been meaning to think of a plan before falling asleep. 'Let's go and have a look at the palace close up – we might see something obvious.' This wasn't his best proposal ever, Emmie thought, but it was worth a try. Quietly, the pair slipped out of the playhouse and walked through the bushes to the lawn at the back of Buckingham Palace.

At the treeline, Emmie stopped and scanned around. It was getting quite dark now, and she couldn't see very far, which meant that they were unlikely to be seen either. Several windows on each of the four floors had lights on, which gave them a chance to see inside easily, whilst staying in the shadows. They slowly walked across the great lawn, heading for the terrace which ran across the width of the palace. Many of the lowest windows had blinds pulled, and the next level up, which were the largest windows, seemed to be the main living spaces. It was possible to see a large piano in one room, and a dining table and chairs in another.

'What's higher up, do you think?' Jack asked. 'Would that be the bedrooms?'

'Probably,' agreed Emmie, 'with the servants' quarters above them.' She craned her neck to see the upper floors. 'Hold on a minute!'

'What? What can you see?' hissed Jack.

'Look up there – who do you think that is?'

Jack stepped back a bit and gazed upwards where Emmie pointed. There was a girl in the window, staring out at the sky and resting her chin on her hands. 'Is that Sarah?' he asked.

Nodding next to him, Emmie suddenly felt like the solution to their problem had just presented itself. 'Could you throw a pebble up to that window?' she asked.

Jack grinned to himself. 'Sure,' he replied, 'you want to get her attention?'

'Yes. Please don't break the window though...'

Jack bent down and picked up a small handful of gravel from the terrace. He sorted through it in his palm, selecting a round stone about the size of a pea.

He weighed it in his right hand, testing for how hard he would need to throw, then looked up, brought his arm back and flung it skyward. Silence. The pebble arced upwards, before slowing and returning to the ground beside him. He tried again, this time choosing a slightly larger pebble. The second throw was better, and the pair could see the girl's surprised reaction as it hit the glass in front of her face, causing her to jump backwards. She almost instantly returned, straining to see where the object which had hit her window might have come from. They saw her head moving around in the light from the room, before she reached up and slid the sash window open with a slight squeak of wood on wood.

Sneaking Around

'Who's there?' came the voice from high up inside the palace. It was easy for Jack and Emmie to see Sarah, illuminated by the light from her room, but much harder for her to see out in the twilight. At that moment, a light in one of the rooms below her came on, throwing an orange glow over the friends, as they stood looking up. 'It's you again!' Sarah said in astonishment. 'How did you get out there?'

'We think we know what happened to the diamond,' called Emmie, trying to make herself heard three floors up, without drawing too much attention to themselves.

'What? Wait there a moment,' replied Sarah, before shutting her window with another loud squeal.

Emmie looked at Jack. 'What do you think she meant by that?'

'She's probably coming down. That, or she's fetching someone to throw us out...' Jack joked, though he did wonder if it might be true. They got their answer a few minutes later, as a light appeared through a door next to where they stood. They shrank back against the wall, unsure who was going to appear.

'If it's a guard, we run – right?' Emmie said quietly. They need not have worried though, as Sarah's face appeared around the door as it opened. She stepped out onto the terrace, looking to see where they had gone. 'Over here,' called Emmie.

'What are you doing here?' Sarah asked, 'and what do you know about the Koh-i-Noor diamond?'

Emmie looked at her – the princess wore a long dress with a cream shawl around her shoulders, keeping out the cool of the evening. 'We're fairly sure your missing guard stole the diamond,' she said.

Sarah's mouth opened wide, and she stared at them. 'Why ever would he do that?'

'I don't know,' admitted Emmie, 'but we saw someone dressed just like him take something from the diamond's safe last night. It's a bit of a coincidence that he went missing and then returned after the diamond had gone.'

Sarah looked thoughtful. 'I can see how he could have done it, but I still don't understand why. All the guards swear an oath of allegiance to the Queen – how could he go and steal her property?' She stared hard at Emmie now. 'How were you able to see this happen? Where were you?'

Jack took up the story now, relating how they had climbed onto the pavilion roof and seen the guard through the ceiling. Sarah's eyes bulged at the bravado of their tale. 'Why did you climb onto the roof in the first place though? Wasn't that awfully dangerous?'

Pausing briefly, Jack wasn't sure how to reply. He couldn't tell Sarah the real reason they were looking for the diamond. Even if she did believe them, they knew it was important not to leave too much evidence of their trip back in time, for fear of disturbing the present somehow.

'We didn't think we'd be able to afford to look around again, so were looking at the exhibits through the glass.' Emmie jumped in and offered the explanation. Sarah seemed satisfied by this, pulling the shawl a bit tighter around her shoulders, and studying each of them in turn.

'What should we do next?' she asked. 'If the guard has taken the diamond, then someone needs to get it back.' Emmie smiled inside – it was like the girl had read their minds.

'Could you show us where his room is?' she asked gently, conscious that this was likely their best and only chance to get inside the palace.

'Oh – maybe we could find it!' exclaimed Sarah. 'The Prince is so angry that the diamond is missing – this would make him very happy. The Exhibition has been his project, and the star attraction disappearing could ruin it.' She turned back to the door and pulled it open again. 'Follow me.'

The first thing Emmie noticed inside the palace was the carpet. It was soft and thickly woven, in a deep red with gold decorative pattern. It led off in front of them, along a wide corridor lit by gas lamps.

'This way,' said Sarah, opening a door in what appeared to be a panelled part of the wall.

'Oh wow. A secret door!' Jack was really excited by this latest development. 'Where does it go?'

'Just up to the top floor, where the servants and guards sleep,' explained Sarah. 'We need to try and avoid meeting anyone, as you're not meant to be here.' They stepped through into a much plainer space, with cream painted walls and a polished wood floor. A set of stairs rose upwards into the darkness ahead of them, and Sarah reached to turn one of the gas lamps on. It flickered into life, casting shadows up the staircase and making a faint popping sound. 'Ok – try and walk slowly,' Sarah advised, 'footsteps echo a lot more in here.' She started to climb the stairs, one hand on the black iron rail as she went.

Emmie glanced at Jack, as Sarah disappeared upwards into the darkness. There was a gentle hiss, then light glowed from the next landing, and they began to follow. Four flights of stairs later, they arrived at a stout wooden door which was closed. Sarah stopped and turned to them, her face looking a little strained. 'We have to be really careful now,' she whispered, 'there's likely to be people around up here.' Even though most of the royal household were still at their duties in the early evening, some of the off-watch guards could be around.

Sarah put a hand on the door handle, slowly turning it. She eased the door open, spilling light from the corridor beyond. As she stepped through, a voice very close by spoke and the door was pulled sharply shut, making both Jack and Emmie jump. Hearing muffled voices through the door, they tried to listen to the conversation in vain - the thick wood obscuring much of the sound.

'What do you think is going on?' whispered Jack, his voice sounding a little panicked at their current predicament.

'I don't know...' replied Emmie. 'I guess she just ran into one of the staff.'

Suddenly, there was a loud thump from the other side of the door, and then silence. A tense moment passed on Jack and Emmie's side of the door. Still silence.

'Should we take a look?' asked Jack. 'We've come this far...'

Emmie nodded in assent. 'Ok, but just open the door a crack first, to see what you can.'

Placing his hand on the door handle, Jack tentatively started to turn it. His heart was racing, and he wasn't sure what to do if there was someone stood on the other side. Or worse...

'Gently,' Emmie reminded him, though he didn't need telling this time.

As the handle reached the maximum rotation, Jack began to ease the door open, a small pool of light appearing by his feet. He leaned forward, putting his eye to the crack and trying to see what was beyond. After some gyrating to find the best position, he looked back at Emmie and shook his head.

She frowned back at him. What did a shake of the head mean? Was it 'all clear' or 'bad news'? She thought to herself that maybe she should have taken the door task instead. A moment later, she got the answer anyway, as Jack opened the door much further and stuck his head out to check in the opposite direction.

'No-one there,' he said quietly.

'And nothing to suggest what the thud was?' Emmie asked, squeezing past to take a look herself. The corridor was completely empty, and nothing seemed amiss. 'Odd,' Emmie remarked, 'very odd.'

She looked at Jack, a baffled expression covering her face. 'Shall we wait to see if Sarah comes back?'

'We could be here all night, and we'll probably get caught,' Jack reasoned. 'I think we should have a look around, since we're up here.' He pointed down the corridor, where a number of doors could be seen. 'Those might be bedrooms – we could check and see if any of them belong to the missing guard.'

'We don't even know which guard it was though – finding the right room is going to be almost impossible.'

Jack looked at her. 'Have you got a better idea?'

She stared back – he did have a point. Doing nothing wasn't going to help them find the diamond. 'Ok,' she said slowly, 'let's go and have a look.'

They moved cautiously out into the corridor, walking slowly so that their footsteps wouldn't be heard. The first door they came to had a small white sign with black stencilled letters on. It read 'Under-Footman'.

'What's an under-footman?' asked Emmie.

'I don't know, but seeing what's on the roads around here, I don't think I'd like to be one,' joked Jack, trying to lighten the tense mood.

The next door had a sign which read 'Footman', and the one after that 'Colour Sergeant'.

'We're getting warmer,' said Jack, 'at least there are some soldiers' rooms along here.' Up ahead, there was the sudden slam of a door, and the sound of footsteps could be heard coming their way. Jack grabbed Emmie's arm – his eyes wide in a mixture of shock and fear. 'In here!' he said urgently, opening the door to the next room along and pulling her inside.

The Wardrobe

They stood just inside the door, listening to the footsteps in the corridor outside. Thud. Thud. Thud. Thud.

'What do we do if they come in here?' whispered Emmie. She looked at the furniture in the room by the dim light still coming in through the window. There was a bed, a wardrobe and a large trunk. 'There's not really anywhere to hide.'

'Shh!' Jack put a finger to his lips. The footsteps were right outside now, and it sounded like they were slowing. They hugged each other, fearful of what might happen next. Jack could feel Emmie's heart beating close to his.

Thud. Thud. Thud. Thud. The footsteps were moving away again now. The pair dared to relax slightly, letting go of each other and stepping apart.

Thud. Thud. Thud. Thud. The resumption of the noise made both of them jump. It seemed to be coming from another direction now. Jack looked at Emmie in confusion. Where was the noise coming from?

'It's over there...' she breathed, pointing into the corner of the room.

Jack's face would have been comical if it wasn't for their situation. He was totally confused — his ears hearing one thing, and his brain telling him another. 'The wardrobe?' he mouthed back.

Thud. Thud.

Emmie nodded. The noise was definitely coming from the wardrobe, and that could only mean one thing — there was someone, or something, inside.

His hand trembling, Jack walked over to the wardrobe and reached for the handle. He shakily tried to pull it, only to find the door locked.

Thud. Thud. The noise was more urgent now — whoever was inside having realised for certain that there was someone else in the room. 'Look for a key,' Jack hissed, scanning the room for a likely location. He ran his hand along the top of the wardrobe in case the key had been put there, then turned his attention to the bed. Emmie tried the trunk but found that to be locked too.

'Where would you hide a key?' she asked him quietly, still not wanting to give too much away to whoever was locked inside.

Suddenly Jack's face lit up, and he walked quickly over to the door. He reached out for the key which protruded from the keyhole, wriggled it, and held it up. 'Hidden in plain sight,' he announced, returning to the wardrobe and inserting it. As he turned the key, they both held their breath, waiting to find out who, or what, was inside. The door swung open to reveal a man sitting on the floor of the wardrobe, bound and gagged. He wore a vest and black trousers, held up with braces, and he looked very angry.

The man strained against the ropes holding his arms and legs together and tried to make a noise through the cloth stuffed into his mouth as a gag. Emmie stepped forward and gently pulled the gag from his face.

'You need to help free me – I must get after him immediately!' he said, struggling once more.

Emmie hesitated for a moment, prompting the man to pull even more determinedly at his captive wrists and ankles. She was in shock at finding the man in the wardrobe, compounded by his apparent level of anger. It was understandable that he was irritated at being tied up, but she felt sure he must see that they were only trying to help him. Jack broke the tension by reaching for the knot by the man's wrists and trying to tease it undone. It wasn't an easy task – whoever had tied the ropes had pulled the knots tight as they did it. The man settled down slightly as Jack worked, no doubt some relief setting in.

'Thank you,' he said gruffly, as the knot finally eased, and he could move his wrists a little.

Emmie stared at him, as Jack finished undoing the knot and his wrists became free. 'What happened?' she asked tentatively.

The man rubbed his wrists, which were red and sore from where he had been struggling. 'I don't know...' he said slowly. 'One minute I was getting undressed, and the next I woke up in the wardrobe.' His hand moved to the back of his head, touching it gently.

'Did you bang your head? Does it hurt?' said Emmie, watching his face as a flicker of discomfort passed over it.

'Or someone knocked him out,' suggested Jack, who had bent down to release the man's ankles.

'I think you might be right,' he agreed, still tentatively exploring his head. 'No idea why though – nothing seems to have been taken. Not that I have much here anyway...'

'Do you know how long you were in there for?' Emmie found it a little too much of a coincidence that they were looking for a rogue guard, and now they had found one tied up. Something felt very wrong.

The man shook his head slowly. 'I came off duty and headed upstairs to get undressed. There was a knock at the door... I don't remember anything after that though.'

Emmie looked at Jack – the man's memory didn't seem to be entirely missing. He'd been able to remember the knock at the door, after telling them that he didn't know what had happened. Jack gave her a small smile of acknowledgement – he had picked up on the changing story too.

'When we opened the door, you said you had to get after someone,' began Jack. 'Who was it?' The man stared at him, seemingly not understanding the question. His ankles were free now, and he cautiously tried to stand up. 'Woah there! Easy.' Jack grabbed at his arm as the man swayed and then sat back down with a thump. His legs had clearly been out of use for many hours. Looking frustrated, the man tried again – this time, Jack and Emmie took hold of an arm each, pivoting him across the room and sitting him down on the bed.

'You need to rest for a bit,' Emmie told him. 'You can't do any good in this state.'

The man leaned back against his thin pillow, seemingly resigned to the need to give his body a break. His shoulders slumped a bit – the earlier fight evaporating from him. 'Where did you come from, anyway?' he asked. 'And what are you doing in the palace?'

Emmie decided that staying as close to the truth as possible was best now. 'We're helping Sarah look for something that's gone missing,' she explained.

'You mean the Princess?' said the man, looking surprised. 'Where is she now then?'

'She went the other way down the corridor,' Emmie said. It was probably true, as they hadn't seen her since she went through the door ahead of them earlier. 'We ought to go and catch up with her really.'

The man shivered a little. 'It's cold in here – would you mind passing me my tunic?'

Emmie gazed around the small room – there was no tunic to be seen. 'Where would it be?' she asked.

'In the wardrobe—' he stopped abruptly, remembering that there had been nothing else in the wardrobe apart from him. His forehead creased, and his eyes narrowed in confusion. 'Maybe the trunk?' he suggested, pulling a small key out of his trouser pocket and handing it over. Jack took the key and went to open the trunk, leaving Emmie sat on the end of the bed. He undid the padlock and swung the lid upwards – inside was a small book, an umbrella and an overcoat, but no tunic.

'It's not in here,' he called, closing the lid again and handing the key back.

Emmie looked at the man again – some things were slowly starting to fall into place for her. 'What's your name?' she asked gently. 'I'm Emmie, and this is Jack.'

'Jefferson,' the man replied. 'Sergeant Augustus Jefferson, though you can call me Gus if you like.'

'So, Gus,' Emmie continued, 'what is your role here at the palace?' She looked at him expectantly – feeling like she knew the answer already.

'I'm part of the Queen's guard,' Gus explained. 'We accompany her when she is outside the palace.'

'I knew it!' exclaimed Emmie, prompting a surprised look from both Gus and Jack. 'Were you with the Queen at the opening of the Great Exhibition yesterday?'

'Yesterday?' replied Gus. 'What do you mean? The grand opening is tomorrow.' He sat up, looking towards the wardrobe once more. 'I'm going to have to find another tunic before then though.'

Emmie took Gus by the hand and quietly explained what she thought had happened. 'The opening was yesterday,' she began. 'I think somebody knocked you out and shut you in the wardrobe so that they could take your place.'

'But who? And why would they do that?' Gus seemed thoroughly confused by what he was hearing.

Taking a deep breath, Emmie continued. 'The Koh-i-Noor diamond is missing, and we think whoever pretended to be you took it...'

Realising The Truth – Part 1

Gus stared at Emmie in horror. He opened his mouth to try and speak, but no words would come out. He looked around the room frantically, as if trying to work out what he should do, then slumped back in despair. 'The Queen's diamond...' he finally managed. 'I should have been there.'

'It doesn't sound like you stood a chance,' offered Jack, trying to make the man feel better. 'If you were jumped from behind, then you didn't even see it coming.'

'But I don't understand how whoever did it managed to get in. This is one of the most heavily protected buildings in London.'

'Maybe someone they knew let them in?' Jack suggested. He caught Emmie's eye at this point and saw her suppress a smile. It had been unexpectedly easy for them to gain access, so it was plausible that someone else could have done the same.

'I suppose...' conceded Gus. 'Why did no-one come to look for me though?'

It was Emmie's turn now. 'Well, Sarah said that the disappearing guard's voice had changed somehow—'

'Hold on a minute,' Gus interrupted her. 'Am I not the disappearing guard? I don't understand what you're saying.'

Emmie looked at him and realised they hadn't started from the beginning. 'It sounds complicated,' she agreed. 'What happened is that four guards turned up with the Queen as expected, then only three were present when it was time to leave.'

'That's how we found out about it in the first place,' Jack added. 'We were standing near the royal party when they wanted to leave, and you could tell there was a fuss, even though no-one actually said anything. It was tense, you know?'

'Eventually, they left with just the three guards,' Emmie finished.

'Leaving the rogue one behind to steal the diamond presumably?' Gus was now catching up fast.

Emmie nodded. 'Exactly. We also went back that night to try and see some of the exhibits when the crowds had gone. There was a man at the diamond safe, doing something by candlelight. He was wearing the same red tunic as the royal guards.'

'My tunic...' said Gus quietly. 'You said a moment ago that this guard's voice had changed somehow too – what did you mean by that?'

Emmie thought for a moment – this was the least obvious part of the mystery. 'I don't know... Maybe the other guard looked like you?' she suggested.

'That would explain why no-one came to find me, I suppose. If the imposter was credible enough, then everyone would have thought it was me.' Suddenly Gus put a hand to his mouth in horror. 'Does that mean I might be suspected of taking the diamond? They'd lock me up forever... Or worse!'

'We need to work out where this other guard might have gone. Finding him is our best chance of putting this right.' Emmie was relieved that Gus was now firmly on-side for helping them, yet worried about what might happen to him if they didn't get it right. She motioned to Jack, who was standing in the corner of the room watching the conversation. 'We should try and find Sarah – she might have seen him.'

'Ok,' he agreed, a little uncertainly, starting towards the door. He listened for a second, trying to hear if anyone was in the corridor outside, without letting Gus realise exactly what he was doing. They needed the man to carry on thinking they were in the palace legitimately. Satisfied that it sounded quiet, he gently turned the door handle and stepped outside.

Taking a deep breath, he turned back in the direction that they had come from earlier, retracing his steps along the corridor. He passed the door that led to the stairs, half-tempted to go back through it, but realising that Gus, as well as Emmie, was depending on him. The corridor seemed to stretch on forever, running arrow straight across the width of the palace.

'What are you doing up here?' The voice from behind caused him to jump out of his skin. Feeling a lurch in his stomach, he stopped and slowly turned around to face a maid carrying a pile of linen. She was wearing a black dress, with a white apron, and didn't look any older than he was. There was an uncomfortable pause, where they both stood staring at each other, neither really sure what to do next. 'You're not meant to be up here, are you?' she said in an accusing tone, seeming to sense his discomfort at being stopped. Jack's mouth went dry, and he tried desperately to think of a creative reason to explain his presence. Seconds ticked by, and the maid started to open her mouth to shout an alarm.

'Jack!' A new voice behind him left the maid's mouth hanging open – her eyes wide in surprise. When the shock wore off, she closed her mouth, hurriedly bobbed down in a half-curtsey whilst still holding the linen, and scurried away.

Jack spun around to see Sarah looking at him with a smile on her face. 'You're not really managing the discreet part, are you?'

'Where did you go earlier?' he replied. 'We heard voices and then a loud thump. When we opened the door, there was no-one there.'

'I met one of the footmen,' Sarah explained, 'I think I gave him quite a shock – being up here. The thud you heard was him dropping his shoe cleaning box. I had to pretend that I was looking for a housekeeper, so he didn't get suspicious.' She smiled at the recollection. 'It seems I'm not the most discreet either.'

'I'm glad I've found you anyway - we've got something to show you. Come with me – Emmie's waiting.' Jack led Sarah back along the corridor, gently knocking on the bedroom door before they entered.

Sarah put a hand to her mouth in disbelief as they entered the room. 'Sergeant Jefferson! How did you get up here? I just passed you on the stairs.'

They all stared at Sarah, before Gus pulled himself to his feet, bowed his head and addressed her. 'Your Royal Highness.'

'There's no time for all that,' said Sarah hurriedly. 'How did you get up here so quickly, and where has your tunic gone?'

'He's been in here all the time,' Jack joined in. 'We found him locked in the wardrobe.'

'What do you mean?' Sarah managed to sound even more incredulous than when she had first entered the room and seen Gus.

Emmie's face suddenly paled, and she let out a gasp. 'He must still be in the palace. We have to get after him!' Behind her, Gus nodded his head vigorously in agreement.

'Will someone please explain what is going on?' Sarah put her hands on her hips, staring at them frustratedly. They seemed to be talking a different language all of a sudden.

Emmie put a hand out to placate the girl. 'We think your missing guard was an imposter, pretending to be Gus – Sergeant Jefferson.' She paused briefly, allowing the revelation to sink in. 'He came into this room, hit Sergeant Jefferson over the head and shut him in the wardrobe, so that he could take his place in the guard detail.'

'Why on earth would he do that?' Sarah was still totally confused. 'Anyway, I've just seen Sergeant Jefferson...'

'Exactly,' continued Emmie. 'You saw his double though – he wouldn't have had time to come up here and get undressed. Besides, he's been with us the whole time.'

There was silence for a moment, the only sound was the chiming of a clock somewhere outside. 'But why?' Sarah repeated quietly.

'To steal the diamond. He must have thought he could get close to it if he seemed to be someone official.'

The pieces were falling into place for Sarah now too. 'I suppose that's why he disappeared when we wanted to leave yesterday. He was probably hiding somewhere until everyone had gone.'

Jack nodded – he didn't want to get left out of this conversation. 'Emmie told me that you'd said the guard's voice was different somehow. I imagine it's easier to make yourself look like someone else than change how you sound.'

Now it was Gus's turn to speak. 'My lady – if you don't mind, I believe we should get after this man immediately. Should he still be in the palace, we stand a much better chance of getting the Queen's diamond back.'

Sarah took a step backwards. 'Of course – that is the most important thing. He was passing the blue drawing room, headed for the kitchens—'

'We must hurry then!' Gus cut across her. 'Begging your pardon, my lady.' He paused for a moment, uncomfortable about talking this freely in front of a princess. 'If he is headed for the kitchens, then I fear he means to leave through one of the back doors. If we don't catch him now, then there is a real chance the diamond will be lost for good.'

19

The Pawn Shop Again

'You can't go out looking like that,' Emmie said, pointing at Gus's chest. The white vest he wore wouldn't exactly fit in walking around the palace, and they didn't need to run into any more complications.

'What about the overcoat in the trunk?' suggested Jack. He walked back across the room, neatly catching the key which Gus threw to him. Bending down to the trunk, he soon had the overcoat out and handed it to the soldier.

Emmie smiled at him. 'That's much better. People know you, and that should help us.'

Sarah took a deep breath and looked a little apologetic. 'I think I should stay here – a princess might be slightly conspicuous walking around London.'

Nodding, Emmie felt a sense of relief. She had wondered how this scenario might play out and didn't want to have to suggest Sarah stayed behind. 'Don't worry – we'll get the diamond back,' she said, trying to sound more confident than she felt.

'We should go now.' Gus led them to the door, nodded a final time to Sarah, and left the room with

Jack and Emmie close behind. As he closed the door, he spoke quietly. 'That man is unlikely to still be in the palace – we should go through the kitchens, but be prepared for us to have to search for him outside.'

*

The sound of voices, muffled by a heavy door, came from the kitchen. A moment later, Gus reappeared, shaking his head. 'He's not been through there.' He looked up and down the service corridor, white painted walls reflecting the light from gas lamps mounted at head height.

'What now?' Jack asked. 'Where would he go?'

'I think he'd look to either hide the diamond somewhere he could come back to or sell it quickly so he could disappear.' Emmie wasn't sure which was most likely.

'He'll sell it,' said Gus firmly.

Emmie stared at him. 'Why are you so sure?'

'People have seen his face now. You worked it out pretty quickly – he won't risk coming back.'

'Ok, then – where would he sell it?' Emmie was relying on them finding the diamond so that Mr Briggs would keep his end of the deal and tell them what he knew. The King was also in need of their help to save his coronation, though he didn't know this of course.

'The pawn shop...' said Jack quietly. 'That's where people sell things, and it's really close by.' Emmie glanced over at him – his face was pale at the recollection of their experience the morning before. For her, it felt like a lifetime ago already - so much had happened since then.

Gus nodded appreciatively. 'Where is it then, lad?'

'Um, not far from the back of the palace.' Jack was sure now that this was where the man would head – he just didn't want to go back. Swallowing his trepidation, he closed his eyes for a minute and then relented. 'We were there yesterday – I can show you.'

Gus led them to the delivery entrance at the back of the palace, and out into a large gravel yard. It was properly dark now – just the street lamps along the wall outside giving any illumination. 'This way,' Gus told them. 'We just need to get through the guardhouse, and then we'll be out on the street.'

Jack stared across the darkened yard. It was hard to see anything clearly, but Gus obviously knew where he was going. 'Won't any of the guards on duty wonder why we're with you?' he asked. In the gloom, he thought he saw Gus's brow furrow as the man realised what he had said.

'Just follow my lead,' Gus said quietly, 'and don't say anything to anyone.' He crossed the yard and approached a large gate, which was firmly shut. To the side was a small door set into the wall - Gus knocked on it once, before opening it. Jack looked at Emmie, wondering if they should just stand and wait. The man hadn't said anything about following him, so it seemed like the right thing to do.

A moment later, the gate opened a crack and Gus appeared from the other side. 'Right. Come on then - no dawdling,' he said sharply, looking at the pair. Surprised, they walked towards him and passed through the gate. He gave them both a little shove as they went, as if to hurry them up. Reaching the other side, Jack saw a red-painted sentry box, complete with a stern-looking guard inside, and then they found themselves on the pavement. The gate swung shut behind them, and the sound of bolts being slid home cut through the still night.

'That way – and don't come back!' Gus pointed towards the main road, where they could see the occasional horse and cart moving slowly by. His tone was still very unfriendly, so Jack and Emmie decided to do as they were told and started walking in the direction he had indicated. Footsteps sounded behind them a moment later, as they passed into a pool of darkness and Gus caught them up. 'Sorry about that,' he said quietly. 'I needed to think of a reason to get you past the guards in a hurry, so I said I'd found you wandering about in the grounds.' He chuckled to himself for a moment. 'Not so far from the truth really.'

Jack turned to the man, nearly saying something sharp in return, but thinking better of it. He was still rattled by the idea of going back to the pawn shop and didn't need any further surprises. 'The shop is just down that road over there,' he muttered. 'Surely it'll be closed at this time of night though?'

'I wouldn't be surprised if our friend has some connections there,' explained Gus. 'He might prefer doing his business when there is no-one else around.'

'So, what are we going to do?' Emmie asked as they moved down the street. She noticed how much harder it was to have a conversation when you could only see the other person's face as you passed a street lamp.

Gus scratched his head thoughtfully. 'Someone should go for the police really – we don't know how many people there might be.'

'No thanks,' said Jack immediately.

Emmie stepped in to explain. 'We had a brush with the police yesterday morning – in this pawn shop actually. It wasn't nice.'

'What happened?' Despite the urgency of their task, Gus was intrigued at this latest revelation.

Jack looked at him uncertainly, trying to work out how much to say. 'Um... We found something and tried to pawn it – the man in the shop said it was stolen and called the police.' He couldn't tell the whole truth, but this was close enough to it.

'Was it stolen?' Gus asked.

'No,' replied Emmie, shaking her head.

'Well, that's alright then.' He thought momentarily, then spoke again. 'Maybe I should go and alert the police – just in case they remember you?' Jack nodded gratefully at this suggestion. They were approaching the drinking fountain that they had stopped at the previous day. A steady drip could be heard coming from the spout.

'The pawn shop is just along here,' Jack explained, pointing further down the road.

'Right, well I'll head off to fetch a policeman. You go and wait near the pawn shop and see if anyone comes out. Whatever you do – don't go inside though,' Gus warned as he left them.

Jack and Emmie crossed the street, keeping close to the shadows in front of the houses they passed. 'How are you feeling?' whispered Emmie.

'Ok, I think,' Jack replied. 'I'm sure waiting outside will be fine.'

The pawn shop loomed up ahead of them, the sign swinging lazily in a gentle breeze. It didn't look any better in darkness – the peeling paint was still visible, and there was an odour of decay. No lights were showing, and it seemed the shop was well and truly closed. 'It doesn't really look like somewhere with enough money to pay for a stolen diamond,' mused Emmie. 'I wonder if we've guessed wrongly?'

'I bet they make loads of money – it just suits them to have a run-down shop, so people don't rob them.' Jack's cynical viewpoint was probably not far from the truth. 'Hold on! What's that over there?' He pointed to the other side of the road where a man was hurrying along and looking around nervously. The man crossed the road in front of them as Jack pulled Emmie back into the shadows.

'He's going into the shop,' she whispered. 'There's definitely something going on – it's too late for normal business.'

'We're just going to wait though, aren't we?' Jack felt his stomach twist a little at this latest turn of events. He leaned on the fence, then stumbled and almost fell as it gave way behind him. 'Woah,' he cried, momentarily forgetting the need to be quiet. The fence swung back behind him and made contact with his shoulder. 'Ouch!'

'It's a gate!' exclaimed Emmie, watching the wooden panel continue to swing gently. In the poor light, the gate blended in with the rest of the fence - Jack must have dislodged the catch when he leaned on it. He saw a glint in her eye and knew what was coming next. 'Now we know there's someone in there, shall we try and see what's going on?'

Closing his eyes and rubbing his temple, Jack tried to decide how brave he was feeling. It would only be peering in somewhere, so maybe it would be fine? Without waiting for an answer, Emmie slipped through the gate, causing Jack to follow her – mostly out of fear at being left alone. They crept around the side of the shop, feeling their way along the rough brickwork in the darkness. Coming to a corner, they saw a small storage yard illuminated in a beam of moonlight, with a large window overlooking it. Emmie couldn't resist peeking in through the window, expecting to see into the darkened shop. However, what she did see was totally unexpected.

Trapped

The window had bars on the inside, making it look slightly like a prison. Emmie reasoned that they were probably there for security, but the temporary flashback to the police cell yesterday wasn't a welcome one. However, it was the room beyond the window which had captured her attention. Through the darkness, she could make out two figures sitting at a table and staring at something between them. They seemed to be talking, and their body language was very animated. In some ways, there was nothing unusual about what she could see, except that one of the figures was wearing a red tunic...

Catching her breath, she nudged Jack and pointed towards the figures. 'I think that's the fake guard,' she said softly.

Jack peered more closely at the scene inside. 'I think you're right,' he agreed. 'Do you think that's the diamond though?' As he spoke, the figure in the red tunic reached out towards the object on the table and cupped a hand over it. This caused even more arm-waving and gesturing.

'We need to hear what they're saying.' Emmie was not going to let the rescue of the diamond slip through their fingers again. 'I wonder if this window opens?'

'It's got bars on – you can see that,' Jack reminded her. 'You'd be better off trying that door.' He pointed to a wooden door on the other side of the yard. It had seen better days, like the rest of the shop, and there was a piece of board nailed across where the glass would have been. Two steps later, and Emmie was across the yard with her hand on the door. She reached for the handle and gently tried it – to her surprise it turned easily. Pushing the door, she eased it open, letting a smell of stale cooking waft out into the night air.

'Come on!' she encouraged Jack, eager to get inside, but not so keen to do it alone. He hesitated, worried about the consequences of getting caught in the building. 'What are you waiting for?' Emmie hissed again. Grudgingly, Jack stepped across the yard and stood beside her.

'Be really, really quiet,' he urged, as she put a foot on the step and entered the doorway.

As she closed the door behind them, taking care not to let it click as the latch engaged, Emmie looked around the room they had entered. It seemed to be some kind of small kitchen, with a range in the corner and a few pots strewn about. There was an archway leading through to a small dining area, and then a door firmly closed at the end of the room.

Silently padding past the dining table, Emmie reached the door and cupped a hand to her ear to listen. She could hear faint voices through the wood – the door obviously led into the room they had seen from outside. There was a keyhole next to the handle, and she knelt beside it in an effort to hear better.

'It's worth much more than that,' came a voice from the next room, slightly distorted by the keyhole. Her eyes widened, sure that the figures behind the door were talking about the diamond. Sarah had been right too – if it was the fake guard talking, then he did sound quite different to Gus. She motioned to Jack, waving him over to join her by the door.

'Take it or leave it,' another voice replied. 'You're not going to find anywhere else to sell it. I bet half of London is looking for this now.' The first voice started again, but Emmie couldn't quite hear what was said. The reaction from inside the room was quite clear though. 'You what? Get out of here!' Heavy footsteps stomped towards the door and Emmie grabbed at Jack, pulling him close to her. She was just in time, as the door was flung open, trapping them in the corner of the room behind it. A shadowy figure strode into the middle of the room, then turned to look back through the doorway. 'I said get out!' he snarled.

Emmie was silently staring from the corner and realised this was the man they had seen in the pawn shop the previous day. She held her breath and kept a grip on Jack's arm, knowing that being found now would likely escalate the angry situation further.

The man moved over to the back door, turning the key and finding it already unlocked. He gave a little grunt of surprise, before opening it wide and issuing a final ultimatum to his companion. 'Go on, or I'll make sure anyone coming after you knows where to look.'

'Ok, I'll accept your terms...' The other voice, who was surely the guard they were seeking, spoke in a resigned voice.

The pawn shop owner paused a moment, one hand on the back door, then slowly closed it and turned the key. 'First sensible thing you've said,' he muttered. 'No-one else is going to touch you, or your stolen diamond. I reckon they'd push for treason if they find you.'

Behind the door, Emmie choked back a gasp. This was it – they'd found the diamond and heard confirmation that it was the right one. More footsteps sounded now – the other person was coming through the doorway into the kitchen too. There was a creak of floorboards as the footsteps passed by and then, to Emmie's horror, the door started to move very slightly – swinging closed by itself. She grabbed at the handle in panic, but only succeeded in hitting it with her outstretched fingertips and accelerating its movement. They stood motionless as their hiding place was revealed – hoping that somehow they would remain invisible.

First, the back of the second man came into view. He was wearing a red tunic, and they could see that it was the same as the royal guards wore. A split second later, the pawn shop man saw them. Almost in slow motion, Emmie saw his eyes narrow in disbelief, then he launched himself across the room and grabbed hold of both of them by the arm. 'What are you doing in here?' he roared, the guard spinning round in surprise at the sudden reaction too. Before either of them had a chance to react, he continued – so close to Emmie's face that she could see the hairs growing out of his nose. 'You're going to regret coming in here – believe me.'

A long moment passed – Emmie and Jack stood stock still, hearts hammering in their chests, whilst the man refused to break eye contact. Eventually, the guard tugged his arm. 'Can't you get rid of them? I want my money.'

'Oh, I'll get rid of them all right – snooping around in my house. It just won't be in the way you're intending.' The man's voice was menacingly cold, and he stepped forward again, causing the pair to flinch. 'Get through there,' he ordered, pointing to the doorway which led further into the house.

Emmie struggled to find her voice – her shoulders shaking with fear. 'Please,' she started, 'I think there's been some kind of mistake—'

'The only mistake that's been made is you coming in here. Now move!' The guard folded his arms and took a step forward too. The odds were not in their favour. Reluctantly, Emmie stumbled through the doorway and into the next room. It had a large table in the middle, with chairs at which the men had been sitting. There was a tattered sofa in one corner, and a fireplace with glowing embers. Jack followed, standing on the edge of a rug, and looking as terrified as he felt.

As the man entered the room behind them, he gestured towards a small door in the opposite corner to the sofa. 'Open it,' he instructed.

Emmie slowly moved across the room, trying to work out how they might get out of this mess. She reached for the door latch and lifted it. The door swung open, letting a musty, damp smell into the room. Emmie could see steps disappearing down and knew what was coming next. A bitter taste rose in her throat as she felt panic coursing through her body.

'In you go then,' said the man, sneering at the pair.

'But please—' she tried again to no avail, her voice rising in pitch.

'Either you go in quietly, or we'll throw you in – simple as that.' The man took another step towards them.

Emmie didn't fancy any broken bones, so decided they were better going quietly for now. 'Come on,' she muttered to Jack, trying to sound brave. 'It'll be ok.' They stooped to go through the door, then carefully descended the steps into the gloom beyond. Halfway down, the door slammed behind them, plunging the pair into total darkness, and they heard a key being turned in the lock. Emmie choked back a sob, then took a deep breath and steadied herself. 'Keep holding the handrail,' she hissed. 'We don't know how far these steps go.' Slowly, they edged further down, feeling for each step until they hit the uneven surface of the cellar floor.

'What now?' asked Jack, an irritated tone in his voice. 'It was all very well coming in here without a fight, but how are we going to get out?'

'Hush a minute,' said Emmie, noticing a small sliver of light in the corner of the ceiling. 'I think that's a vent – we might be able to hear what they're saying still.'

'So what?' Jack retorted. 'Listening doesn't get us out of here.'

'They were bigger than us – sometimes you have to fight smart,' explained Emmie. 'Gus has gone for the police, which means they'll be here soon. It's better that we listen and see what else we can find out which might help to get them locked up.'

'I'm fed up with this diamond!' snapped Jack. 'All it has done is get us into trouble. I don't even care about the coronation - I just want to go home now.' He stomped off sulkily into the darkness, leaving Emmie to investigate on her own.

Realising The Truth – Part 2

The light from the vent cast a faint glow around the cellar – enough for Emmie to see that it was largely empty. It had probably been used as a coal store, as there seemed to be some small, stone-like objects piled up in one corner. There wasn't enough light to tell much more, but at least she could move around without tripping over anything.

There was a scraping sound from above, and then a murmur of conversation could be heard filtering through the bars of the air vent. The men must have sat down again to conclude their business. Emmie worked herself into the corner under the vent, trying to catch what was said. It was difficult as the sound was distorted, but she managed to hear some of the discussion. 'Need to conclude this business and get out of here… Fair price… Got me over a barrel…'

'It sounds like the pawn shop man is driving a hard bargain,' she whispered to Jack. It wasn't surprising – the guard would likely have very few options of people who he could sell the diamond to. 'Jack?' she said questioningly, remembering that he had gone off in a sulk.

'Over here,' he replied, from somewhere on the other side of the cellar. 'I think I've found an opening.' He sounded a lot happier than a few minutes before. Reluctantly, Emmie dragged herself away from the fragments of conversation and carefully picked her way across the cobbled floor.

'What have you found?' she asked, after almost bumping into him in the gloom.

'Can you hear that?' Jack said – the faint noise of footsteps coming from over their heads.

'Is it inside the house?'

'No – feel the draught coming down. It must be a coal grate set in the pavement.' Jack was sure they could find a way to climb up and release the grate to escape. Before Emmie had a chance to respond though, there was an audible shout from upstairs in the house.

'I'm going to creep up the stairs and see if I can hear better. We can try and get the grate open after that,' she suggested.

Jack's initial excitement fell flat. He understood why Emmie wanted to gather some evidence on what had happened with the diamond, but he didn't like being trapped in the cellar. Didn't like it one bit. 'Ok,' he said quietly, 'I'll wait. I think this is our best way out though.'

Giving his shoulder a little squeeze, Emmie cautiously made her way back to the staircase and climbed up it. The stone steps made no noise as she ascended, but they were damp and slippery, causing her to hold onto the handrail firmly. As she reached the top, the voices were much clearer, and she was surprised to hear a third person speaking.

'Come on, brother, we should be gone... It must be dark, for we are too conspicuous otherwise...' It sounded like someone had come to join the guard and was urging him to hurry.

'He drives a hard bargain, Gus – we need the best price...' The guard's words in reply sent a cold shiver down Emmie's back. Gus was in the room – what was he doing there? It certainly didn't sound like he had brought the police with him...

'Take it or leave it – that's the deal, just like I said before.' The pawn shop man let out a harsh laugh. 'You'd be foolish not to take it too.'

'Gus – what do we do?' The guard spoke in an exasperated voice, knowing they had been forced into a corner.

Then Gus spoke again, and any lingering doubts Emmie might have had evaporated. It was definitely the man they had rescued, and who was now meant to be returning with the nearest policeman. She wondered how they had managed to be so completely taken in. 'We've got to take it, and get out of here before someone comes,' he said.

'Right then. If you're decided, I'll go and count it out for you.' The pawn shop man still had a trace of laughter in his voice, and Emmie could imagine how irritated the two other men must be at his attitude.

As he left the room, his footsteps echoing on the bare floorboards, she heard Gus speak quietly to the guard. 'We have to be quick, brother – there's a boy and girl who saw you with the diamond and have been sniffing round.'

All of Emmie's senses jangled at this point – she obviously hadn't mis-heard Gus call the other man 'brother' earlier. They must have been in it together from the start. What's more, it was only a matter of time before the guard realised the boy and girl locked in the cellar might be the same ones who Gus was referring to... She listened as hard as she could to the conversation, trying to make sure she didn't miss anything.

'Saw me? Where did they see me? How do you—' The guard's questions were cut short by the pawn shop man noisily returning.

'Right. So we have ourselves a little problem here. Takings haven't been great this week, and I'm going to have to offer you a little less I'm afraid...' There was an awkward silence, where Emmie presumed the men were all staring at each other, working out what to do next. She touched the rough wood of the door, as if it would somehow help her to see the scene on the other side.

'You double-crossing swine!' bellowed the guard suddenly, making Emmie jump and grab onto the rail beside her. There was a scuffle outside the door, and she could hear multiple thuds, along with grunts from the men as they fought each other. She flinched with every blow – it was really unpleasant listening to the fight, though it was serving as a good distraction to anyone remembering that they were in the cellar.

She heard Gus speak again, his voice sounding duller than before. 'Just take the money, and let's go before it's too late!' There was another thud-like sound, and then the jangling of coins being dropped into a bag. Heavy footsteps crossed the room outside the door, then paused.

'What about those children?' she heard the guard say. 'Can they identify us?'

Behind the door, Emmie's heart skipped a beat, and a chill spread through her body. This was it – the moment it all came tumbling down. Once the brothers realised that they had both seen her and Jack, the pair would be in real trouble.

'Well, they've seen me – and worked out that you're my double,' confirmed Gus. 'I don't know where they've got to though – they were skulking around outside earlier.'

The guard's face clouded as he started to join the dots together. 'What did you say they looked like?'

'A boy and girl – both around twelve I'd say. He had a cap on, and she had plaits.'

'We found a couple of children like that earlier. They were inside the kitchen – we thought they'd broken in.'

'Where are they now?' Gus sounded worried at the prospect that Emmie and Jack may have learned more than he'd thought.

'In the cellar,' the guard replied. There was a sharp groan as his foot connected with the pawn shop man's prone figure. 'Where did you put the key?' he demanded. Some more shuffling and groaning ensued, before Emmie heard him take a step towards the cellar door. 'Got it,' he said triumphantly.

Emmie's head whirled – what should she do? There was no easy way out of the cellar – even if they could dislodge the coal grate and climb up, it would still take time. Time they didn't have. She considered rushing out as soon as the door was opened, but then realised she would be leaving Jack behind.

'Jack?' she called quietly down the stairs. There was no reply. She tried again – as loud as she dared, for fear of being heard through the door. Descending a couple of steps, she called him a third time, but still without a reply. Her anxiety levels were through the roof – feeling literally trapped and now alone too. Deciding her only real option was to hide, she quickly went down the remaining steps onto the uneven stone cellar floor.

Having been in the dark for a while now, her eyes were more accustomed to it, and she could make out an internal wall running across the cellar. On one side was the air vent she had listened at earlier, whilst on the other was the coal grate which Jack had been so keen to find a way out through. The side with the air vent was darker and would make the better hiding place. She wondered where Jack was though – it wasn't that big a space, and he should have heard her calling, quiet as it was.

She jumped at the squealing sound of a key in the door behind her – the noise travelling down the steps with a menacing tone. 'Jack!' she called again; this time less worried about being overheard. 'Where are you?' There was no answer, save for the sound of the door being wrenched open, throwing a shaft of light out which illuminated her like a rabbit in headlights. There was nowhere to run now.

It was pointless, but Emmie darted to her right, trying to melt away into the remaining darkness. She glanced back at the doorway and saw a figure in red standing at the top of the stairs. The guard stared down into the darkness. 'You can come out now,' he called, laughing unpleasantly. Emmie stood still, pressed against the damp wall and wondering what had happened to Jack. She couldn't call out to him now as she might give away what little cover she still had. She watched the guard – he seemed reluctant to come down into the cellar, maybe as there was no light and he wasn't sure what he might find.

'Whatever you're going to do, get on with it.' Emmie recognised Gus's voice from the room beyond. She flinched – what was the guard going to do? He was obviously worried about them having seen his face.

The guard grunted, then put a tentative foot forward into the cellar. He came down a couple of steps, the view in front masked by his shadow. Then everything seemed to happen in slow motion – suddenly the guard was cartwheeling down the steps, and there were raised voices from the floor above. Different voices. A figure peered through the door, waving a lamp in front of them, then slowly began to descend the steps. As they reached the bottom, Emmie tried to press herself further into the wall, without success. She held her breath, terrified of what might happen next.

'Miss? Where are you?' called a man's voice. Emmie carried on holding her breath, wondering how long she could do it before she might faint. The man swung the lamp in an arc ahead of him, then everything went black.

Saving The Day

Jack looked up towards the grate, feeling the cool air on his face. If he squinted, he could make out a smudge of light through the grate, though it was hard to judge how high it was in the darkness. How was he going to get up to it? Feeling with his foot, he tried to work out if the wall was rough enough to give him a toe hold. The brickwork was old and uneven, but it wasn't really suited to climbing.

He leaned back against a brick pillar and look upwards again. As he stared, his feet found a groove in the wall and an idea began to form in his mind. If he braced himself against the pillar and the groove, he might be able to edge upwards towards the grate. It had to be worth a try.

Tensing his shoulders, he pushed backwards, and tried to lock his legs out straight at the same time. He shuffled his feet in a walking motion up the wall, managing to raise himself to about shoulder height before his calf muscles began to burn. Frustrated, he dropped down to the floor, rubbing his legs and wondering how far he would actually have to climb.

Jack could hear some of the angry conversation from upstairs and was determined to try again. They had to get out of this cellar, and the only way he could see that happening was through the grate. He screwed his eyes up, leaned back into the wall and tried again. This time, he got within touching distance of the grate. It wasn't actually so far up after all, and he managed to poke two outstretched fingers through the bars and into the night air before his legs gave way again.

Spurred on by the fact that it was definitely possible, Jack took a deep breath and inched himself upwards for a third time. Touching the grate again, he pushed with his fingertips, trying to move the metal cover somehow. The grate held fast - it was never going to be that easy, was it? Jack tried to think whilst holding himself up against the wall – that wasn't easy either. After a moment, it came to him – maybe the grate twisted to open?

Slowly, he wriggled both arms upwards, trying not to move his shoulders as that would make him fall. He grabbed hold of the grate and tried to turn it in a clockwise motion. It remained stubbornly stuck. He tried again – this time turning it the other way – and was rewarded with a screech and some definite movement. Feeling elated, he turned it further, sensing the cover becoming free. Suddenly, one edge lifted, and he pushed as hard as he could, sliding the grate aside. Above him, he could see a few stars twinkling through the murky sky, and realised he needed one more burst of effort to escape.

Inching painfully higher, with each movement causing his leg muscles to burn even more, Jack managed to get an arm out of the hole above him. He grasped around for something to pull himself up with, but there was nothing in reach. Grunting again, he raised the other arm, desperately trying not to alter his position too much, for fear of falling back down. Bracing his arms against the sides of the opening, Jack heaved. This was a dangerous move – he had to shift his weight from his legs to arms but avoid doing so too early. As his arms took the strain, he felt his legs turn to jelly and realised how close he had been to them giving in.

Pulling himself up, his head emerged through the hole, and he got a view of the empty pavement. Thankfully, the street was deserted, as his appearance might have caused some suspicion. He pulled harder, reaching for a drainpipe on the wall nearby, and finally emerged, breathing heavily, onto the path. He rolled to the side, leaning against the wall to catch his breath. He was going to have to find a policeman, as it seemed that Gus hadn't been able to.

Jack slowly got to his feet and wondered where he might be able to find a policeman. He could walk back to the police station they had been taken to before, but the thought of even seeing that building again made him shudder. No – it would have to be somewhere else. Playing the previous day over in his mind, he suddenly remembered that the policeman who had arrested them outside the pawn shop had come from further down the road. It might be a coincidence, but it was probably worth talking a walk to see He'd have to be quick though, if he was going to save Emmie, the diamond and the coronation.

Thrusting his hands into his pockets, he walked quickly away along the road, half-turning once to glance behind him. It didn't feel great to be getting further away from Emmie, but she needed his help, and this was the only way. He passed a couple of people on the other side of the road, walking in the shadows, and quickened his pace even more. Up ahead, the houses were thinning out as the city gave way to the suburbs. He gave a cursory look down a side street on the left, then stopped and rubbed his eyes. Was that a glimmer of blue further down the street?

Deciding that the blue glow was worth investigating, Jack changed direction and hurried towards it. As he got closer, he could see that it was a lantern mounted above a doorway. His heart leaped – it was a police station! As he approached, he saw that the door was shut, and the windows appeared to be in darkness. The relief he had experienced a moment earlier washed away as quickly as it had come, and he stared at the darkened building. He wondered what

Emmie would do in the same situation, and then realised that he knew exactly what that was.

Striding over to the door and hammering on it with his fists, Jack shouted as loudly as he could. 'Help! Will someone help?' There was no reply, just the echo of his shout gently fading away. He tried again, banging in a mix of frustration and helplessness. If no-one answered, how was he going to help Emmie and save the diamond? By the time he had found another police station, the diamond would be long gone, and he dreaded to think what might have happened to Emmie. There was still no response, and Jack felt overwhelming despair. He sat down on the pavement outside the police station and tears started to roll down his face. He had failed – it was as simple as that.

After a couple of moments feeling sorry for himself, something pricked Jack's conscience. He might be out of ideas, but he was sure his friend wouldn't give up this easily. Whatever the situation, Emmie would stubbornly stick it out. Gritting his teeth, he tried again, this time noticing a small light in one of the upstairs windows. 'Help! Help!' he called, pounding on the heavy wooden door.

Above him, a window slid open, and a man's head leaned out. 'What do you want?' he said sleepily.

'My friend... Trapped... Stolen diamond,' he managed, the words coming out in a tangled mess. The last words got a reaction from the man though.

'What did you say?' he called, sounding more alert now. 'What's that about a diamond?'

'We found the stolen diamond,' Jack said, hoping that this man was actually a policeman.

'Wait there. Don't move,' ordered the man, sliding the window shut and disappearing. Jack wiped the tears away from his face and stared up at the window, noticing the curtains still flapping with the man's hasty exit. A moment later, the door opened in front of Jack and the man stood there, hastily buttoning up his dark blue police tunic. 'What do you know about diamonds then?' he asked, fixing Jack with a stern stare.

Jack paused before answering, then it all came tumbling out. The Exhibition, the fake guard and the stand-off at the pawn shop. 'You've got to help my friend too,' he urged, 'she's trapped in the shop with the thief.'

The policeman's stare had moved from stern to incredulous by this point. 'That's quite a story,' he said, narrowing his eyes.

'It's true. It's all true,' pleaded Jack. 'Please hurry, or we might be too late. They had agreed a price for the diamond when I left.'

This seemed to make the difference for the policeman, spurring him into action. He opened the door again behind him and shouted some orders. A few moments later, another man appeared, also hastily pulling on his tunic. He picked up a wooden truncheon from inside the door and pulled it closed behind him.

'It's this way,' said Jack, pointing back up the street. 'And turn right at the end.' The two policemen set off at a fast walk, with Jack struggling to keep pace with them. As they rounded the corner, he pointed up ahead. 'That's the pawn shop there – you can see the sign.'

They reached the shop and Jack indicated the gate to the rear yard. 'You wait here,' the first policeman ordered. 'We don't need you getting mixed up in a fight.'

'But—' Jack started to protest, before being met with the kind of look which told him not to argue any further. Sulkily, he leaned against the wall of the shop as the policemen eased open the gate and disappeared from sight. Seconds later, he heard shouting and the sound of breaking glass. There were quick footsteps behind the shop – someone was running down the passageway towards him! The gate was wrenched open, and a figure appeared, turning in Jack's direction. Instinct took over and he stuck out a leg as the figure passed him, sending them sprawling onto the floor. He saw in horror that it was Gus he had tripped up – the man's face now bleeding from the impact with the pavement. 'Gus! I'm so sorry...' he began.

Before he had a chance to say anything further, one of the policemen rounded the corner and leaped onto Gus, pinning his arms behind his back. 'Not so fast!' he said breathlessly.

'But that's Gus – he was helping us...' Jack said, the words dying in his throat as he realised what was happening. There could only be one reason that the policeman was chasing Gus – he was working with the impersonator.

The policeman looked up at him as he slipped a pair of handcuffs onto Gus's wrists. 'He's definitely in on it,' he said, confirming Jack's thoughts. 'Come on – let's go and find your friend.' He led Gus back around the shop, with Jack following closely behind. They entered through the door at the back, and Jack headed straight for the cellar door.

'She's down here!' he said urgently.

The Aftermath

'Emmie!' a distant voice called to her. It was like someone was shouting at her from across the street and underwater at the same time. 'Emmie,' it came again, sounding slightly less muffled this time. What was going on? Then Jack's face swam into view in front of her, bathed in the warm orange glow of an oil lamp held by a policeman standing right behind him.

'Jack?' she said weakly. 'Where were you?'

'Someone had to get us out of here,' he grinned. 'I thought I'd shift that grate whilst you were up there listening at the door.' He paused for a minute, and she saw that his face was streaked with black coal dust. 'It wasn't too hard actually and, when I popped out, I found a police station close by. Convincing them what had happened was the tricky part though...' He put out a hand to Emmie, helping her to her feet. 'Let's get you back upstairs – I think you'll be pleased with how it's worked out.'

They slowly walked up the steps together, Jack leading the way, and emerged back into the room with the large table. Emmie blinked in the bright light, then blinked again at what she saw. There had obviously been a ferocious fight before Jack had arrived with the policemen – all of the chairs were smashed and there was a big hole in one of the walls. Lined up alongside the window were three men in handcuffs, guarded by an angry-looking policeman and looking very sorry for themselves. As she looked at them in turn, Gus refused to meet her eye. He stared stubbornly at the floor in front of him, and she wondered if he felt a little bad about how they had been treated in the end. His brother, on the other hand, glared angrily at them, clearly fuming about how his plans had unravelled. She stared at the pawn shop man, who had a black eye and one arm hanging limply by his side. He must have come off worse in the fight – the brothers not impressed by his low offer for the diamond.

The diamond! Suddenly, Emmie remembered the point of why they were all there. 'Did you find the diamond?' she asked the policeman who had come down into the cellar nervously, hoping it hadn't slipped through their fingers once again.

'Oh yes, miss. Don't you worry about that,' he said, patting his breast pocket which she could see was bulging. 'They're sending a special wagon to take this safely back to the station.' He opened his notebook and took out a pencil, before looking expectantly at her. 'I'm going to need a statement miss, if you'd be so kind.'

Jack leaned over and whispered in her ear. 'We should try and get out of here now. The diamond is safe, and we shouldn't mess around with time any more than we need to.'

Emmie nodded slowly in agreement. He was right – they knew all too well what could happen when you changed something in the past that wasn't meant to be changed. They'd righted something which was wrong, and now it was time to go. She smiled sweetly at the policeman, clearing her throat before she spoke. 'There's not a lot to say really...'

'Go on, miss,' he encouraged her.

'Well, those two men,' she pointed at the guard and pawn shop owner, 'shoved us into the cellar and locked us in. We didn't really see anything after that.'

'How did you get in here in the first place?' asked the policeman.

A plan started to form in Emmie's mind. 'Let me show you,' she said, winking discreetly at Jack. 'We'll just need to go outside.' She led the way to the door and stepped out into the yard. As soon as they had both cleared the doorstep, she grabbed Jack by the arm and pulled him in the direction of the street. 'Run!' she urged, dodging along the passageway, dragging him behind her.

As they reached the pavement, she quickly looked left and right, deciding on a whim that left might be better. They raced along the flagstones, dodging around streetlights and the few pedestrians who were still about. After a few hundred metres, she risked a look behind them, then gratefully slowed down. Jack pointed at a side street, and they turned down it, hoping they had put enough distance between themselves and any pursuers. Chests heaving with effort, they looked at each other, then descended into hysterical giggles as the adrenaline coursed through their bodies.

'What now?' asked Jack through his laughter. 'Do you think we can go home at last?' It had only been a few days, but their latest adventure had felt like a lifetime, so much had been packed into it.

Emmie stared at him - the oversize cap was still somehow stuck on his head, even after squeezing out through the cellar grate. He looked even more ridiculous now, with his coal dust-streaked face. It would be good to get home, and also to see if Mr Briggs kept his promise to explain why these adventures kept happening to them. She thought for a minute – they ought to be sure the diamond was where it was supposed to be before they went back. 'How about we visit the Exhibition again in the morning, just to check the diamond is safely back?' she suggested.

Jack wiped the back of his hand across his face, streaking the coal dust even further. 'I suppose so,' he said, slightly reluctantly. 'We don't want to get home and find that things aren't back to normal after all. Plus you've got the coronation to look forward to,' he added.

Emmie took a few steps back to the main road and looked towards the pawn shop. 'They've come for the diamond,' she said quietly, pointing down the road. A horse-drawn police van was visible outside the shop – dark in colour and pulled by a single horse. As they watched, another van came slowly along in the other direction – this one looking unpleasantly familiar.

'Is that the one we were in?' Jack muttered, looking down at his feet. The recollection of their troubles the day before dampening his pleasure at having rescued the diamond.

'Come on.' Emmie put an arm around Jack's shoulder and led him off in the opposite direction. She sneaked a look behind her and saw the three men being led out of the shop and into the police van. Smiling grimly, she picked up the pace a little and tried to distract Jack. 'Where are we going to sleep tonight?' she asked. 'We still don't have any money...'

He looked across at her as they passed underneath a streetlight. 'Maybe the park again? Those benches weren't so bad.' They forked off to the right, heading towards the side entrance to Hyde Park once more. Jack felt a little brighter as they left the visible reminder of the pawn shop behind and started to think about the next day. 'They had some railway inventions in the Exhibition,' he said, 'I'd quite like to look at them before we go back.'

'Sure, why not,' replied Emmie as they reached the park gates. 'It's not like we're coming back here again.'

Jack looked up at the wall they had climbed previously. 'Want to give me another leg up?' he asked. 'Maybe next time we'll end up somewhere easier to get around...'

The Diamond Returns

Jack stretched as he woke up on the park bench, seeing the sun rising over the city to his left. The sky had a grey tinge to it as usual, and the orange sunlight filtering through made it seem like the sky was on fire. He put his hands behind his head and lay there for a while, thinking about the last few days. Victorian London wasn't for the faint-hearted, and living with no money was really difficult. He was glad they were going home - back to television, school and normality. 'Emmie,' he said gently, 'are you awake?' There was some stirring on the next bench, and then Emmie blinked, before opening her eyes properly.

'Have you been awake long?' she asked, rubbing her eyes.

'Just a few minutes,' Jack replied. 'It's really peaceful – quite a contrast from how it'll be later when the crowds arrive again.' His stomach rumbled, making him grin. 'Time for some food too, I think.' He remembered the sausage stall from the day before – handing out free breakfast to the workers – and suggested to Emmie that they try again today.

'Good idea,' she said, nodding. 'We might see Bert too – it would be nice to thank him for helping us.'

Together, they walked across the dewy grass and headed for the pavilion, which appeared to be deserted still. Jack paused to rub the coal dirt from his face with some wet leaves, earning a thumbs up from Emmie over his improved appearance. As they got closer to the entrance, they could see that the doors were closed, and a heavy chain hung between the handles. 'That's odd,' remarked Jack, 'there were people setting up around this time yesterday.'

'Let's sit and wait,' Emmie suggested, looking around the empty park. 'I doubt they'll want to stop people coming in and lose the ticket sales.' Retreating back to a discreet distance, the pair sat down by a tree and waited to see what would happen next. There was a steady stream of traffic on the road outside the park – a few carriages, but mostly the horse-drawn omnibuses which seemed to carry everyone around this city. The repetitive clip-clop of hooves on cobblestones was quite soothing, and Emmie found herself trying not to doze off.

Jack, on the other hand, had an eye trained in the distance, watching the road past Hyde Park Corner. He could see a number of people on horseback, riding alongside a covered wagon. It stood out as a bit unusual this early in the morning. As he watched, the convoy turned along Knightsbridge in their direction.

He nudged Emmie, who was half-asleep at this point. 'Look! Are those soldiers riding alongside that wagon?'

Emmie squinted into the distance - the riders certainly appeared to have red tunics on. 'I think so,' she agreed. A moment later she gave a sharp intake of breath. 'What if they're bringing the diamond back? It would certainly explain why the Exhibition is closed still.'

They watched together in silence for a moment, the riders and wagon coming ever closer. As they reached the park entrance, a man appeared from behind the wall and unlocked the heavy black gates. He slowly swung them open, pushing hard to get them moving, and allowing the riders to enter the park. The wagon followed and swung round on the gravel in front of the pavilion, great wooden wheels making a crunching sound as it did.

Two riders jumped down from their horses and walked quickly to the rear of the wagon. One unlocked the faded black door, whilst the other swung it open. Jack could see bars inside – it looked like some sort of cage. A flash of anxiety hit him as he realised it was probably a police van most of the time – used for transporting those who had been arrested. Swallowing nervously, he watched as the first man leaned into the wagon and brought out a small metal box. He locked it to his wrist with a pair of handcuffs. 'They're not taking any chances this time,' Jack said quietly to Emmie. The box must contain the returning diamond – there was surely no need for such security over anything else.

The two men walked towards the pavilion, with the remaining guards dismounting and joining them. They reached the entrance, removed the chain, and eased one of the giant doors open, disappearing inside.

Jack turned to Emmie, who was still staring at the glazed entrance. 'What are you thinking?'

'I'd really like to know the diamond is back where it should be before we try to get home,' she answered. 'I know it's probably in that box, but I really want to hear what Mr Briggs promised to tell us. I need to know why we keep going back in time.'

'Ok...' said Jack slowly. 'I think there is a way.'

Emmie looked back at him, hope building in her eyes. 'How would we get inside with all those guards around?'

'Remember Bert's secret passageway? We can use that – we only have to get through the door and then we'll be hidden from view.'

A big smile broke out over Emmie's face, and she gave her friend a hug. 'Well done – I'd forgotten about that. It's a great idea!' She got to her feet, offering him an arm and pulling him up too. 'Let's go.'

They crept cautiously towards the pavilion, keeping the wagon between them and anyone who might be watching from the door for as long as they could. Not wanting to crunch across the gravel, they skirted the sweeping arc in front of them, favouring the grass instead. When they got close to the edge they walked around, coming at the pavilion from the side. There was a thin strip of grass edging the flower border around the glass structure, and they carefully walked along this to arrive at the main entrance. Ducking down and peeking through the window beside them, Jack confirmed that the pavilion looked empty – the guards presumably all down at the end with the diamond display. Quickly looking around to confirm they weren't being watched, he reached up for the door handle and silently turned it.

'Come on,' he urged Emmie, 'let's keep it quiet though.' They slipped through the door, gently latching it behind them, and emerged in the tree-lined entrance hall. It was somehow even more majestic without anyone around – the full scale of the structure being on show. Jack pointed over to the curtain which Bert had taken them through into the secret passageway. 'Best get hidden in case anyone comes,' he said.

'Oi! What are you doing?' A shout rang out just as Jack was holding the curtain back for Emmie to pass through. He quickly ducked behind too, then let the curtain drop back into place.

'Did they see us?' whispered Emmie, moving carefully down the narrow passage.

'I think they must have done,' replied Jack. 'Just stay quiet though – I'm sure it'll be alright.' There were hurried footsteps the other side of the thin stand wall, which stood between them and their pursuer. They both stopped and held their breath, trying not to move a muscle as the person outside walked back and forth, likely confused at where they had disappeared to. A sneeze began to build in Emmie's nose, and her eyes widened in fright – surely there was no way of disguising the sound that was about to erupt? She tried everything that she could think of – swallowing, touching the roof of her mouth with her tongue, and pinching her nose – but it still kept on coming. Finally, she crouched down in a ball on the floor, put her face in the crook of her arm and tried to smother the noise as it came out. Pfft! She looked at Jack, who was still listening hard, then tried to refocus on the footsteps outside. They were fainter now, and still moving – that was good, as it must mean the person hadn't heard her sneeze.

They waited in silence, not daring to show their faces in case there was still someone prowling around looking for them. After a few minutes, more footsteps sounded – this time there were several people walking together. Jack put his eye to a crack in the wooden wall and peered out. 'The soldiers are going,' he said quietly. They marched out in line, carrying the metal box which he presumed had been used to transport the diamond. As the soldiers exited the pavilion, a stream of workers took their place – keen to get their tasks done before opening time.

'Do you think it's safe to look now?' Emmie asked.

Jack nodded, thinking they would probably blend in with the workers, as they had before. He led the way further along the passage, behind the Indian spice stand and out to the small exit by the refreshment room. As they emerged back into the daylight, he couldn't help noticing how the sunlight danced across the glass roof. It was easy now to see why this building was referred to as the 'Crystal Palace'.

Walking quickly across the transept to the diamond display, Jack felt a rush of excitement as he saw something sparkling inside the security cage. 'Is that the right one? Has it been put back?' he asked Emmie.

She bent down to look at the sparkling gem, though she already knew the answer. 'Yes, it's the right one,' she breathed. There was an almost hypnotic quality to this diamond – the way it sparkled and caught the light was entrancing.

'Ah – I thought I might find you here.' A familiar voice from behind them jerked Emmie out of her trance, and the pair turned around happily.

Would You Like To Know The Truth?

'Bert!' Emmie cried, rushing over to the boy and giving him a hug. 'I'm so pleased to see you.'

Bert's cheeks went very pink, the colour then spreading down onto his neck and almost matching the red necktie he wore. 'You've seen it's back then?' he managed, still looking a little uncomfortable. 'They say one of the palace guards tried to steal it.'

'Not one of the real ones—' started Jack, then paused as Emmie jabbed him sharply in the ribs. This wasn't the time for explanations.

'I mean, surely not a real guard – that would be terrible.' Emmie tried to cover for Jack's impulsive statement. Luckily for her, Bert still seemed flustered at her unexpected attention.

'So, how come you're back again?' he asked them. 'Are you looking for a job?'

Emmie grinned, tucking a stray strand of hair back behind her ear. 'No, we thought we'd come for a last look around. We're going home tomorrow.'

'Oh... right,' said Bert, disappointed. He had hoped these new friends might stay for a while.

'But we couldn't go without saying thanks to you for all your help.' Emmie paused for a moment, wondering how much she could say. 'You helped us a lot with talking to Princess Sarah, and that climb up onto the roof the other night was out of this world.'

Bert was just about to reply, when a man's voice called over from the direction of the refreshment room. 'Come on Bert – you've got work to do!'

Bert sighed and rolled his eyes in the direction of the voice. 'Nice meeting you,' he said. 'You were really interesting.' He then thrust his hands into his pockets and slowly walked off across the floor and back to work.

*

'Do you want to look at those railway inventions you were talking about?' Emmie asked Jack as they walked back through the pavilion, the first visitors of the day filing in through the doors. 'Now the diamond is back where it should be I'd like to get home, but we can spend a few minutes looking on the way out.'

'Sure thing,' he answered excitedly. It was kind of funny, looking at old things which were actually new, especially seeing everyone around them so excited by the technological progress. The railway section was about halfway back to the main entrance, and quite close to the Indian spice stand they had walked behind on so many occasions. It made quite a change to see it from the front – multi-coloured spices set out in an assortment of jars and dishes, all giving off an intoxicating aroma.

They reached the first railway exhibits, Jack eagerly peering up at a giant, green steam locomotive, resplendent with gleaming brass pipework. Emmie sat down on a bench and sighed contentedly – the last few days had been a whirlwind of adventure and emotion, and she felt relaxed for the first time since they had arrived.

'Hello Emmie.' The voice made her jump, jerking her back to the present – or at least the sort of present. She turned and saw Mr Briggs at her side, smiling kindly. 'You've done well – both of you,' he said, sitting down.

'Does this mean we're done?' she asked quietly, searching his face for a clue as to the answer. Now they had solved the mystery of the disappearing diamond, all she could think of was how much she wanted a warm shower and a comfortable bed.

His smile broadened, and Emmie's hopes began to rise. 'The diamond is back where it belongs – both now and in your present,' he told her. 'Once again, you've both adapted to your new surroundings like you belong here.' A flash of horror must have passed across Emmie's face, because Mr Briggs hurriedly assured her that they weren't meant to stay in 1851.

'Oh, thank goodness,' she said in relief. 'I don't think Jack would have liked that very much either!'

'Where has Jack got to?' he asked her. 'I promised you an explanation, and I suspect he will want to hear it as well.'

Emmie's heart started to beat a little faster – she was desperate to find out the reason that these adventures kept happening to them, and now it felt within reach. She glanced at the green locomotive where Jack had been a moment ago, knowing that he was as keen to find out too. 'He was just looking at the railway engines for a bit. He'll be back soon.'

'Ah yes, I can see him. Over there by the signals.' They both stood and waved at Jack, who eventually noticed them and came wandering back.

'This stuff is amazing,' he said, 'there's so much of it too.' He looked at Mr Briggs, a sense of anticipation flickering over his face. 'Are we going to find out what's been going on now...?'

Emmie nodded at him. 'Yes, I think we are. Mr Briggs is going to share that explanation with us, now you're back.' She swung around towards the great glass door at the front of the pavilion. 'Should we walk back to the museum – or at least where it should be?'

Leaving the magnificent structure for the last time, Emmie paused in the midst of the crowds outside to take a final look. The sun was high enough now to be making the whole building shimmer and sparkle, in stark contrast to the soot-blackened buildings surrounding the park. 'I'm glad we saw it,' she murmured, 'it really is very beautiful.'

*

Walking back towards the suburb which, in the present, housed the museum, Emmie found herself still surprised by how many horses were on the road. It was odd to see a traffic jam of animals, all waiting to move forward a lot more patiently than the people in charge of them. Today, there seemed to be more omnibuses than wagons, and the pavements were full of families. She wondered if it might be the weekend – that could explain the large crowds outside the Exhibition too. The constant stream of horses contributed significantly to the unpleasant aroma in the air. It was a heady mix of horse droppings, coal smoke and open drains, and there seemed to be no getting used to it either. It was certainly one thing she wouldn't miss about the 1850's.

'When's the big reveal then?' Jack asked. He was walking slightly in front of them, eager to get back to the present but intrigued by the secrets Mr Briggs had promised to share. He looked at the man expectantly, hoping that it would be worth the wait.

Mr Briggs glanced around them at the crowded pavement, then smiled kindly at Jack. 'Probably not the best place,' he advised, 'let's get slightly further out of town first.' Jack pulled a face but fell in alongside them and carried on walking.

Soon, they reached the large townhouse which stood where they knew the museum to now be. It was close to the pavement, with a narrow garden behind iron railings. Jack stopped in front of it and turned to the others. 'This is it, isn't it? I guess you'll have to tell us now. There are less people around too.'

Mr Briggs leaned against the railings and looked at them in turn. 'Now, this is very important,' he began, speaking quietly and standing close to them. 'You cannot mention what I am about to say to anyone. You have a special gift and can use it for good if you let me help you.'

Emmie's eyes widened, and Jack stared at the man. A special gift? This sounded like more than just a series of time-travelling accidents.

'When you stepped off that bus and found yourself in 1940,' he continued, pausing a moment whilst a group of women walked past, one pushing a pram with large, squeaking wheels. 'Something unusual happened. You passed through a gap in time, and I think you might have been exposed to some special energy when that happened.'

'Go on...' said Emmie softly. This was getting beyond her comprehension, but it did go some way to explaining why things kept happening to them in particular.

'Whatever it was,' explained Mr Briggs, 'it has given you the ability to exploit other gaps in time.'

'So, we can time travel wherever we want? Cool!' Jack was already working out how he could put this new knowledge to good use — maybe they could go back and meet the dinosaurs? That would be some story to tell.

'Not exactly. It's complex - but essentially, if there is a gap in time, you two are much more likely than most to be able to pass through it.'

Emmie thought for a moment. 'You said earlier that we could use this gift for good if we let you help us? What did you mean by that?'

For the first time, Mr Briggs looked a little nervous. He cleared his throat before he spoke again. 'My role is to help resolve things which go wrong through time. I don't have the gift that you do, so by helping me, you can solve problems that I encounter. Think about last night — you saved a valuable treasure from falling into the wrong hands, and ensured the coronation could go ahead as planned. That's a great thing. And also helping save Mary on board Titanic — she was able to do a lot of good in the world thanks to you.'

'So, what happens next?' Jack asked. 'Are we going to have more adventures? How do we find you when we're ready?'

Mr Briggs gave a little chuckle. 'Oh, you'll have more adventures for sure. Next time there's a problem that needs solving, I'll find you. Don't worry about that.' He reached out a hand and patted them both on the shoulder in turn. 'Now, it's time for us to go back to where we each belong. Can I ask you to close your eyes briefly?' Seeing that they both had, he continued. 'Then turn around and open the door to the museum.'

'The what? But the museum isn't there!' said Jack, opening his eyes, then blinking in surprise as a large, red London bus swept up to the kerb beside them. He swung around to see the blue-painted fire door of the museum ajar in front of them. 'How did you—' he started, whirling around again to look for Mr Briggs, but the man was nowhere in sight. 'Where did he go?' Jack asked Emmie.

'The same place as usual I expect,' she replied with a wry grin, 'but I've got no idea where that is.' Looking up, she noticed the Union Jack bunting still flapping in the breeze. 'I think everything really is alright,' she smiled happily. 'It looks like Mr Briggs was right about the coronation!' Emmie reached out a hand to Jack. 'Come on – we'd better get inside and make sure that diamond really is back where it should be though.'

*

A week later, Emmie stood outside Westminster Abbey with her parents and Jack, eagerly waiting for a glimpse of the King as he passed by in his golden carriage. There was a murmur from the crowd further along the road, followed by some loud cheering. Slowly, a row of soldiers on horseback appeared, followed by the carriage itself. Jack looked at Emmie and smiled.

'Looks familiar,' he said quietly. 'Let's hope none of the guards disappear this time!'

Emmie stared, enthralled, as the procession stopped outside the Abbey for the King to disembark. He stepped down from the gleaming carriage to walk inside, accompanied by more cheers from the crowd. He then disappeared from sight, before reappearing on the giant screens which had been erected either side of the entrance, walking slowly down the aisle.

As he took his seat on the ornately decorated throne to the side of the altar, a page entered from the side, carrying a sparkling crown on a purple velvet cushion. He stood patiently beside the King, waiting for the moment when the archbishop picked up the crown and placed it on the King's head. As if on cue, a ray of sunlight lit up the inside of the Abbey, casting a dazzling light from the huge gemstone on the front of the crown.

Emmie put her hand to her mouth in awe. 'I know we did it now! That's definitely the Koh-i-Noor diamond,' she whispered. 'I've never seen anything else sparkle quite like that before.'

As the bells rang out to signify the crowning moment, Emmie turned to Jack once more. 'I wonder where Mr Briggs will need our help next time...?'

'Or when,' he said with a grin.

For The Curious...

The Koh-i-Noor Diamond

The Koh-i-Noor diamond is one of the largest cut diamonds in the world and weighs over 105 carats. It is part of the Crown Jewels of the United Kingdom.

The early history of the diamond is difficult to trace, but it is thought to have originated in what is now India. The stone passed through many different owners, before being given to Queen Victoria in 1849. It was displayed at the Great Exhibition in 1851 with an advertised value of £1-2m – an enormous sum for the time.

Interestingly, the diamond has only been worn by female members of the British royal family, and today is on public display in the Jewel House at the Tower of London.

As with many precious items, there have been conflicting claims as to the Koh-i-Noor's ownership, but I wanted to introduce it in this book as it was the undoubted star attraction at the Great Exhibition.

Sarah Forbes Bonetta

Sarah Forbes Bonetta was a princess of the Egbado clan of the Yoruba people in West Africa. She was orphaned as a child, and later given as a 'gift' to a British Royal Navy captain – Frederick E. Forbes – on Queen Victoria's behalf.

The Queen was captivated with Sarah's intelligence and raised her as her goddaughter in British society, bringing Sarah to such high-profile events as the wedding of her daughter, Princess Alice.

Sarah developed a chronic cough as a young girl in the damp climate of London, and was sent to school in Freetown, Sierra Leone, before returning to Britain a few years later.

She married James Pinson Labulo Davies, a Nigerian businessman, in 1862 and they moved back to Africa to start a family. Sarah had three children, and named her first daughter Victoria, after the Queen.

The Crystal Palace

The Crystal Palace was a glass and iron building, originally erected in Hyde Park, London to house the Great Exhibition of 1851. It was 564 metres long, 39 metres high, and was three times larger than St Paul's Cathedral.

After the exhibition, the structure was relocated to an area of South London called Sydenham Hill and a nearby residential area was renamed Crystal Palace after it. This was also where Crystal Palace football club was formed in 1905 – the team initially playing their games in the grounds of the building.

Many events were held in the Crystal Palace over the years, including the world's first aeronautical exhibition and the world's first cat show. It was also used as the first site of the Imperial War Museum after the First World War.

Sadly, on the evening of 30th November 1936 the Crystal Palace caught fire. Despite 89 fire engines attending the blaze, it proved impossible to put out and the building was destroyed.

About The Author

Glen Blackwell lives in Suffolk, England. He has a career in finance and *The Disappearing Diamond* is his fourth book. Inspired by bedtime reading with his three daughters, Glen loves to bring stories to life for young readers.

Glen would love to hear what you thought about *The Disappearing Diamond* – please contact him as below:

www.glenblackwell.com

Facebook.com/glenblackwellauthor

Twitter: @gblackwellbooks

Instagram: @gblackwellbooks

Alternatively, please leave a review on Amazon or your favourite online bookstore so that other readers can see what you thought.

Thank you!

Readers' Club

It would be great if you would like to join Glen's Readers' Club. Sign up to receive a free eBook at **www.glenblackwell.com/readersclub**

You will also be the first to hear about Glen's new books and get the chance to become an advance reader for new titles.

If you are under 13 then please ask an adult to sign up for you.

Follow Glen

Facebook.com/glenblackwellauthor

Twitter: @gblackwellbooks

Instagram: @gblackwellbooks

More adventures with Jack and Emmie...

www.ingramcontent.com/pod-product-compliance
Lightning Source LLC
LaVergne TN
LVHW091544060526
838200LV00036B/702